A Remote Chance

Adria Townsend

TOWNSEND AVENUE BOOKS

Copyright 2015 by Adria Townsend

All rights reserved. This book or any portion thereof may not be reproduced or used in any manner whatsoever without the express written permission of the publisher except for the use of brief quotations in a book review.

This is a work of fiction. Names, characters, places and incidents either are products of the author's imagination or are used fictitiously. Certain areas or events may have been used as a basis for some of the work, but they are not meant to conform 100% to history.

Published by Townsend Avenue Books

ISBN 978-1515189527

Cover Photo: Copyright Richard Gillard at www.istockphoto.com

Chapter One

One thing after another had delayed the demolition of the old cabin, and another problem was on its way. Thane McMasters could hear it coming in a hurry down the isolated dirt road that dead-ended here on the shore of Garnet Lake. There was no hoping the vehicle would just pass by. He took off his cap as he waited, rubbed the sweat from his forehead with the hem of his T-shirt and tugged the cap back firmly on his close-cropped brown hair.

Jack Hanson had just climbed into the seat of his beat-up old bulldozer after they'd finished replacing a hydraulic line, and he was impatiently motioning for Thane to get out of the way. The old-timer had been around heavy machinery all his life; he couldn't hear the revving of the vehicle's engine or the screech of the undercarriage as it bottomed out in the ruts. But when the horn began to blare, he stopped chewing the lump of tobacco in his cheek and he turned.

"What the hell is it now?" he muttered, as they watched a black Jaguar skid around the last curve and get mired in the soft ground 30 feet away in front of a storage shed, exactly where the dozer had been stuck for most of the morning and into the afternoon. Jack gave an unsympathetic laugh.

The Jag's driver let up on the horn, spun the tires, gave up and got out, leaving the door open and the engine running. Thane could tell she was a down-stater. The car was a sure giveaway, never mind the color, and the way she drove it. He could also tell by the way she dressed in a knee-length skirt and a shimmery top, again in black, and the way she wore her dark hair done up in a tight, uncompromising style. But it was the urgency of her walk that would have given her away without all that and the direct way she approached them, the lack of a greeting.

"You can't do this!" she said.

"Says who?" Jack asked.

"I'm Grady Henderson. You can't do this," she repeated.

"Who's gonna stop me?" Jack said.

She answered his question by stepping over to the corner of the cabin and wrapping her arms around the weathered post that supported the roof of the porch.

Thane blew out a breath. "Ms. Henderson," he began, trying to keep his voice level. "We've got a job to do here."

Her eyes flicked over the cabin. Thane followed her gaze to the hewn siding and the rusting green tin roof that was showing spread along its ridge. The place had been neglected all winter. The water had never been shut off, and the full pipes had burst at the first freeze and leaked until the shallow well had run dry. Why suddenly just a week shy of Memorial Day did Grady Henderson care so much about it now?

"Could you please step out of the way?" Thane said a little louder this time. He took a deep breath, took a step closer and raised his voice so there could be no doubt she heard him. "If you don't leave, Ms. Henderson, I'm going to have to involve the authorities. You're trespassing on—"

"You're trespassing," she said.

"As far as I know Richard Hartwell owns this property."

"It belongs to me! In trust. Richard Hartwell is the Trustee," she said.

"And he's contracted with Sterling Construction."

"Well he shouldn't have!"

Thane blew out another breath. "That's something you're going to have to work out with him. But right now, I'm asking you one more time to leave the premises. If you don't, I'll have you removed."

"And I'll have you fired."

Thane laughed. He didn't technically work for Sterling Construction. Cal Sterling was a good friend of Thane's, but not the best business man. Thane had loaned him money to get through a rough patch, but the patch kept getting rougher. And Thane had ended up working for Cal for free to keep the company limping along and to protect his own investment.

Thane was about to turn away when Grady Henderson's hand shot out and she grabbed the front of his grey T-shirt just under the collar.

"Please," she said and her tone was suddenly different, her hazel eyes darkening along with the lake as the sun ducked behind a cloud. "What's your name?" she asked urgently.

"Thane McMasters."

"Thane, please, I can't lose this too. I just can't. Can you understand that?"

He understood she had a Jaguar and the means that went with it. If she'd lost something already, she still had gained more than most of the people around here.

"Please," she said again. "I'll give you everything I have if you help me."

"I am trying to help you," he said. "You need to get out of the way of this dozer." He put his hand over hers to remove it.

"How much'll you give me?" Jack demanded from his seat on the dozer.

Grady Henderson named a sum that surprised even the birds. Everything was quiet for a long moment.

"You got it on you?" Jack asked.

"Well, not exactly. Not right now."

"How soon can you get it?"

"I could borrow it."

"You don't have it, do you?" Jack said.

"I do! As soon as I come into my trust, I'll give you what I promised and more."

"And when will you come into this trust of yours?"

"When I'm 25."

"Well, how old are you now?" Jack demanded.

"Twenty-three," she said after a pause.

Jack snickered, then leaned over the side of the dozer and spat.

Grady looked away from him and out to the waters of the lake. She seemed to have realized she lost the negotiation, but her posture was more rigid than ever, her hold on the post even tighter.

Thane patted the back pocket of his work jeans for his cellphone. Glancing once more at Jack, he took himself reluctantly out of the path between Grady Henderson and the dozer and strode quickly to his truck. He found the phone on the passenger side of his old Ranger, underneath the sleeping excuse for a golden retriever. He couldn't get reception right here, but if he got farther out from under the trees there was a chance. He pushed the dog, now half-awake, out of the truck.

"Keep an eye on things, Beau," he said, and then he turned his head to stare hard at Jack. "Don't do anything 'til I get back."

"I haven't done a thing in three weeks now. What makes you think I'm gonna start now?" The mean smile that bared Jack's tobacco-stained teeth told Thane he was just itching to start something.

"Trust fund" was more than just a combination of words, it was a physical thing that caused people's eyes to go hard when they heard it. It had that much power, but money still couldn't undo the last seven months.

Grady tried to ignore the dozer driver's curses and concentrate on the waves instead. Every summer they would play a different song against the bulkhead when she arrived, as if the long winter had taught them a new tune. Now all she heard was 'trust fund, trust fund' repeat itself in the water's sloshy rhythm.

Her thoughts were as hard to hold as those waves. Could this be temporary insanity? Or clarity? A cloud finished its slow migration across the sun and the water turned a searing blue in the new light. The picture was so sharp it seemed to cut her. This place was like it had always been, but nothing was the same.

Hartwell had told her the cabin needed some renovation. Grady had planned to drive the four hours north from Long Island after work to see the progress herself. She'd left repeated messages with Sterling Construction for two weeks and every call had gone unanswered until today. The message on her cellphone said the demolition was behind schedule because of mud season, but would be taken care of by this afternoon. Demolition?

She'd left the insurance company where she worked without notice, without logging out of the website she was designing, and made the four-hour trip to Garnet Lake in two, after being stopped twice to be ticketed for speeding. She still should have had time to come up with a plan to stop the demolition, but the shock of the news had left her numb. She knew she had to get to the cabin. She couldn't lose that too. Beyond that she had trouble thinking.

The dozer driver's voice was getting louder. "If this thing don't come down, I don't get paid! First I had to wait for the snow to melt so we could get back here, then I brought the dozer in because Cal Sterling said he couldn't wait another day. Then the rain came and I had to wait two weeks for this mud hole to dry up enough to move this damned thing." His voice kept rising. "I ain't waiting now for some downstate princess who sits around on her trust fund all day and doesn't know what it's like to work for a living. For the last time, are you going to let me get my damned job done?"

"You've got to stop this," Grady said.

"Honey, we're just getting started," he said and then she couldn't hear him as the dozer started with a rattle.

The dog that had been sitting between her and the dozer scuttled backwards away from the machine. Grady closed her eyes. She couldn't move. Her heart had nowhere to go.

Cell service was spotty out here. Thane found if he stood at the end of the dock jutting off the warped bulkhead into Garnet Lake, he could just get a signal. The dock had been left out over winter, and ice floes had crushed the aluminum supports on one side. It was precarious, like this whole situation. Thane turned with his back to the deep water to keep an eye on Jack. Beau sat between the dozer and Grady Henderson, turning his head back and forth, tail thumping happily the whole time.

Thane wiped the sweat from his brow with his forearm and dialed the phone for the third time. This time he got a scratchy connection to State Trooper James Oplin, or Opie as he was known to his friends.

"Just scare her off, Opie," Thane barked into the phone after he'd explained the situation. "I don't want this blowing up."

"What blew up?"

"Just get here as quick as you can," Thane said before the call was lost. He wasn't sure what Opie had heard. He was pretty sure he didn't understand what was going on. Hell, Thane wasn't sure he himself understood it.

He watched the scene in front of him. Jack was sputtering, but the dozer was still quiet. Thane walked quickly to Grady Henderson's Jaguar, reached inside the open door and killed the motor. That's all he needed was a brush fire. The tourist train in North Creek had already started one on its trial run. Spring had been wet, but short. The sun had come on too strong and there'd been a burn ban in place for a week.

The contents of Grady Henderson's purse were strewn all over the driver's seat, and the ground. He slammed the car's door shut. As he turned, sunlight reflected on the small square of window on the storage shed nearby and caught his eye. Or was it movement inside the shed?

Thane took a step towards it, but stopped mid-stride as he heard the dozer's engine wheeze back to life. He could tell Jack put it in reverse, just by the squeal of gears. And he turned just in time to see the machine lurch back a few feet.

Jack wouldn't do it, Thane was saying to himself, even as he started running. It's just an empty threat, he tried to convince himself as Jack was yelling a high-pitched warning to Grady. Thane was close enough now to see Jack wrench the lever into first gear, and the tracks of the dozer start to spit dried mud. The gears whined and then slipped as they so often did in that dangerous old machine jerking it forward.

There was no time to move Grady Henderson gently out of harm's way. Thane tackled her, breaking her grip and landing on top of her in the dirt with a thud that was drowned out by the dozer crashing into the porch post where she'd been standing. Without a support, the corner of the roof came down like a guillotine just inches from Jack's face.

Thane would have liked to take a swing at him himself, but it looked like Grady was beating him to the idea. He had eased his weight off her, expecting her to be dazed, but she sprang up towards Jack instead. Jack would have deserved everything he got, but Thane had the feeling he'd give back even worse. Grady Henderson didn't know what she was getting into.

Thane grabbed her by the wrist to stop her, and she turned on him and swung blindly with her free hand and missed. Spinning her on her own momentum he caught her up with her back to his front in a tight hug, pinning her arms to her body. But it wasn't enough to hold her. Her head snapped back, and he could tell she'd split his lip.

Jack jumped from the machine, his ragged baseball cap in his hands. "I swear, I just meant to scare her."

"Get the hell out of here, Jack," Thane said through clenched teeth as he changed his position to leave one arm around Grady's waist. With the other hand he held her head back against his shoulder.

"Let me go!" she demanded as she kicked a heel hard at his shin.

He moved his leg out of the way, lost his balance and they both fell again, into the same depression they'd made the first time. He didn't remove his weight from her. It was easier to hold her this way.

"Let me go!" she said again.

Beau had stopped barking. He stood inches from Thane's face, snarling!

With the growling and Grady's protests and the howl of the dozer's motor, Thane never heard Trooper James Oplin pull up to the scene. But it was with relief, he finally saw the polished boots of his friend appear in his field of vision. He could tell Grady noticed it too. Instantly the fight went out of her. She relaxed. So did Thane. And then he made a huge mistake. He let her go.

"Put your hands on your head," Opie barked.

Thane stood up. He didn't bother to brush himself off; he wouldn't know where to start. He watched Grady stand up shakily looking with open expectation from Opie to Jack.

Opie repeated himself. "Put your hands on your head, I said."

Thane could tell Grady didn't know the state trooper was speaking to her. "Wait!" he said, but it was too late. Opie was already too close to Grady, reaching for her arms.

The next thing Thane knew, his best friend was bleeding from the nose and Grady was face down in the mud again, this time with Opie's knee in the small of her back. He was cuffing her with the expertise of a bull-rider tying up a calf. And then he raised his head and put the back of his hand gingerly to his nose. It didn't do anything to stop the bleeding.

Grady was struggling to get up. "What the hell is happening?" she asked.

"That's what I'd like to know," Opie said. His words sounded like they were coming through a tube.

She got up on her knees and Opie pushed her back down. "Stay where you are, damn it."

"He tried to kill me!" Grady said.

"Who?"

She jerked her head in Jack's direction. "Him."

Opie looked up at Thane. "Care to explain?"

"He tried to run me over with that bulldozer," Grady interrupted, trying again to struggle to her knees.

"I wasn't talking to you!" Opie barked at her. "Well?" he looked at Thane again.

Thane flipped off his baseball cap, rubbed the back of his head with the same hand. "I don't know where to begin."

"Start with your lip. It's bleeding."

"So's your nose."

"She do that to you too?" Opie asked.

"I did not!" Grady said. "Did I?"

Thane looked away. He didn't know what to say. Richard

Hartwell, the Trustee of Grady Henderson's trust, was one of Sterling Construction's few paying clients, and its biggest. The situation had been bad enough before Opie had shown up. Criminal charges were not going to make things any better. Any dreams Thane had of Cal Sterling paying him back were going up in smoke. He tugged his cap back on.

"Well?" Opie was asking in a nasally rasp.

"You smell that?" Thane asked. He could swear he caught a whiff of smoke on the still, dry air.

Opie grunted. "I can't smell nothing but blood."

Thane's eyes moved over the landscape, and came back to settle on the storage shed. The door was slightly ajar. Had it been like that before? As he watched, a flame flicked through it. For the second time that day he was running. He reached the shed and slammed the door shut. It was hot, but not hot enough to burn him yet.

Grady Henderson took it all in from ground level. The state trooper was calling in fire on his radio. Thane McMasters was reaching into the passenger side window of an old pickup and emerging with a fire extinguisher, and yelling orders at the dozer driver to do the same. Then the trooper was dragging Grady back towards his cruiser, opening the back door and pushing Grady inside.

"We don't have time for that, Opie," she heard Thane yell.

"If it's arson, I'll make time for it," he snarled, as he slammed the door.

The window pane on the side of the shed burst outward as if punched by a fist of flame.

How quickly things could explode!

Grady felt the pinch of her shoulders, the chafing of the cuffs on her wrist. Oddly enough for the first time she felt balanced. That wasn't a good thing. It meant the powerlessness she'd felt inside since that day in October, was now matched on the outside.

It took a long time for the fire trucks to come trailing slowly after their quick sirens and she worried that the flames would spread to the trees and then the cabin. She couldn't bring herself to believe the cabin would be brought down by a dozer or any other means. The porch the driver had wrecked could still be fixed. She didn't care about the car that was so close to the burning shed. Richard Hartwell had picked it out for her because he had a friend at the dealership and he'd paid for it with the trust. She'd never wanted it, or liked it.

Grady watched the volunteer firemen pump the water out of the lake and onto the burning shed. She noticed the trooper hang back now, bending low over the brush beside her car. He circled it once then stooped to pick something out of the grass. He studied it for a minute then looked up towards her. As he put the object in his shirt pocket, a wide grin dissolved into a grimace of pain as his hand went to his bloody nose. Grady looked away.

After a long while the fire trucks left. The trooper opened the car door, closed it and sat for a moment before turning the key. He put the car in reverse, made a three-point turn and began reciting the Miranda rights in a sing-song fashion as he pulled away.

Grady craned her neck to see Thane push his dog into the cab of his pickup and follow them. And then she saw Jack Hanson hop back up onto the seat of his dozer.

"No!" she called out, but the word only echoed back to her in her muffled prison.

She turned her face away as the dozer bit into another piece of the cabin.

Grady Henderson looked at the judge in the tiny courtroom in the tiny town of Garnet Lake. Justice Michael Mullens stared back.

"Well," he asked. "How do you plead?"

"I didn't do anything," she started, but was interrupted by a grunt from the uniformed man next to her, who was holding a blood-stained rag to his nose. She glanced warily in that direction. So, she had done something, namely broken the nose of State Trooper James T. Oplin. But in her defense, she hadn't meant to.

She looked away from those black angry eyes to Thane

McMasters standing on her other side. He was studying the oak paneling of the judge's raised platform, his arms crossed. His sand-colored hair was cut short, bringing out his solid jaw and cheekbones, making his profile seem rigid. She tried to reach out to him to get his attention, but her hands were cuffed behind her back. She nudged him with an elbow instead.

"Tell them your dozer operator tried to kill me."

He turned to her warily. Brown should have been such a warm color, but his eyes were distant, if not exactly cold.

"He's not my dozer operator, he's an independent contractor. He said the gears slipped." Thane McMasters turned his eyes back to the seemingly fascinating oak paneling.

The judge pushed his reading glasses back up his nose and looked down at the paper in front of him. "Let me read the charges…again. Trespassing, vandalism, arson, assault, resisting arrest."

"I can explain…"

"I'm not looking for an explanation," the judge said in a tired voice. "It's almost 9:00 pm. What I'd like is a plea, so I can go home and finally have dinner. If you won't enter a plea, I'll have to do it for you. It's simple, Ms. Henderson. Guilty or not-guilty. We'll try this one more time. How do you plead to trespassing?"

"That cabin belongs to me. Richard Hartwell's name is on the deed but as a trustee for ME."

The judge sighed. "I'll enter a plea for you of …"

"Not guilty," Grady interjected before it was too late. "Listen, Hartwell told me the cabin was being renovated. I only found out today it was supposed to be demolished. I came up to put a stop to it."

"By vandalizing it and burning it down?" the judge asked as he wrote something on the paper in front of him.

"I didn't set fire to it!"

"But you did to the outshed."

"Why would I do that?"

The judge shrugged and held up a book of matches. "Is this yours?"

It was the kind of matchbook given out as favors at weddings.

Grady nodded glumly.

"Would you mind telling me how you got it?" he pressed.

"I picked it up at a wedding last week."

"Whose?"

"You can read can't you?"

"I'd like to hear you say it."

Grady gritted her teeth. "It was my mother's wedding. . . to Richard Hartwell."

"So Richard Hartwell is the Trustee of your fund and he's also your stepfather."

"Hartwell's my mother's husband; he will never be my father."

"This doesn't look good Ms. Henderson," the judge said.

"Anyone could have stolen the matches from my purse. My car was unlocked."

"You were two miles down an isolated dirt road, who could have done that? Was it bigfoot? Why would he have left your money and your license? And the car?"

"Maybe bigfoot can't drive," she said sullenly.

The trooper next to her gave an angry snort, then growled in pain.

The judge continued. "So to the arson and vandalism charges, you plead..."

"Not guilty!" Grady said quickly.

"What about assault?"

"Oplin surprised me. I thought he was going to arrest the man who tried to kill me. When he put a hand on me, I just lashed out. It was instinctive."

"It was ASSAULT," the trooper snarled.

"You started it," Grady said in her defense.

"And I'll finish it."

Grady appealed to the judge. "Did you hear that? He just threatened me."

"And I'm warning you that I'll add contempt of court to these charges in a minute," the judge said. "How do you plead to resisting arrest?"

"Not guilty," Grady sighed.

The judge addressed Thane. "How much is that shed worth that burned?"

Thane shrugged. "Hard to say what was in it, but to rebuild it, probably $3,000."

"$10,000," Oplin said.

"$5,000, tops," Thane responded.

"There was a boat in there. That's got to be worth another ten grand," Opie said.

"It was a rowboat, probably from the '80s. It's not worth a thousand," Thane countered.

"Two grand at least!" Oplin spat back.

The judge pounded his gavel against the oak desk and the sound ricocheted through the small courtroom. "Gentlemen, this is an arraignment not an auction." He paused for a moment. "Ms. Henderson, what do you think that shed was worth?"

"To me it was priceless."

"I'll set bail at $50,000," the judge said after a pause.

"What?!" Grady gasped.

"That's pocket change for someone like you," Oplin said.

"Do you have the funds?" the judge asked.

"Not on me at the moment. In my trust, I guess."

"When can you get them?"

"When I'm 25."

"If you can't post bail," the judge continued, "I'll have to hold you at the Warren County Jail." He looked at the trooper. "Jim, you're off duty now, who do we have who could make the run to Lake George?"

"It would be my pleasure to escort this...Ms. Henderson to jail," Oplin said with a sneer that made him grimace with pain.

"I am not going anywhere with him!" Grady protested.

"Oh, yes you are!" the trooper responded.

But Grady wasn't, because at that moment the scanner on Oplin's belt began to squawk. The robotic language was mostly unintelligible, but even she could make out the words 'bus' and 'accident' and 'Northway between Garnet Lake and Minersville.'

The judge was standing up, addressing Oplin. "You go ahead, I'll follow in a minute."

The courtroom was small, but that wasn't the reason Trooper Oplin bumped into her as he stormed out. She stumbled on the broken heel of her shoe, and would have fallen if Thane McMasters hadn't righted her.

"Hey," Grady called after the trooper. "At least uncuff me."

Oplin turned on her. To her surprise, he spun her around and uncuffed her. Again she was spinning, and just as quickly she found herself cuffed again, this time her hands in front. He was gone before she could protest, taking the keys with him.

She looked at the judge. "Let me guess. You're the fire chief?"

"And coroner," he responded soberly.

"And undertaker too?"

His face turned even more dour than she thought possible, and she knew she'd guessed right. She also knew she'd gone too far. But she didn't care.

"I should send you to the Warren County Jail pending bail," he said.

"Go ahead," Grady said smugly knowing a town this small wouldn't have the personnel to do that, unless the judge drove her himself the 30 miles down the Northway.

"Instead I'm remanding you to Thane's care until further notice."

Grady's outburst came on top of Thane's. "You can't do that!" they said at the same time.

"I just did," the judge said as he gathered up his papers. He held up her driver's license. "I'll hang onto this for the time being until this matter gets straightened out," he said, tucking the license into his shirt pocket. Then he turned to the door behind him.

"I'll sue you!" Grady called out after him.

He looked back just for a moment so she could see the broad smile on his face. "Go ahead ... if you can find an attorney foolish enough to file the papers. Just do me a favor; turn the lights off when you leave."

"This has got to be a joke," Grady Henderson said.

Thane was not laughing. He held the door to the courtroom open for her, and she hobbled past him. He flipped the light switch, turned the latch on the door and let it lock behind them.

The forecast had promised heavy downpours by midnight and it had already started to rain. At his truck from the passenger's side, Thane cleared the front seat of his tools.

"Move it, Beau," he said as he pushed his old retriever to the middle of the cab. There was no way to explain to this mutt there was no reason to be excited.

He turned to Grady. She was watching him. The uneven lighting in the parking lot made deep shadows under her wide eyes against her pale skin. Or it could have been dried mud, or bruises. The rain was forming dark pearls against her black hair, which was a mess. She started to shiver and he pulled his flannel work jacket from the cab and put it around her shoulders. It must have been a trick of the light that made her look helpless. If he needed a reminder of how able she was to help herself, all he needed to do was think about his split lip which had started to throb.

He took hold of her elbow and guided her into the pickup. The fight seemed to have gone out of her, at least for now. But he'd thought that before and been wrong. While he tried to figure out how to get the seatbelt on her without pinching her cuffed arms in it, the rain worked its way down the back of his T-shirt. It took him awhile to get the belt to latch because nothing worked right in this truck and because he had to constantly push Beau's curious nose out of his way.

Thane avoided the Northway and drove the rutted back way around Garnet Lake, not because the bus accident might have closed it, but because he didn't want his best friend to see who he had in the car with him.

The radio in the truck no longer worked. The only sound in the cab was the whine of the wipers and Beau's rumble of contentment as Grady rubbed the dog's ear. Thane wondered if she even realized she was doing it as she stared out the window.

When he pulled into his dirt drive off the long gravel road, he started to wonder if she wasn't in shock. He got out, opened the passenger's side door, unlatched the seatbelt with some difficulty and stood aside. She didn't move.

"You need to get out," he said. And she did, with his help.

"It's pretty steep, watch your step," he said. She didn't.

He caught her before she tumbled and he didn't let go until they were inside his cabin.

He eased her down onto the wooden boot bench and bent down to take her shoes off. They might have once been black. Now they were mud-brown, one heel was missing altogether. Grady Henderson didn't once look around. She stared straight ahead, holding her head high, while he knelt at her feet like a damned prince charming.

He got up, shed his own boots, led her up the winding stairs to the loft to his bed. Beau eased himself down at the foot of it like a guard.

"I can't sleep here!" she said.

"I'm sorry if it's not up to your standards, but according to the judge it will have to do."

"That's not what I meant," she said.

Thane didn't care what she meant. He went back downstairs, showered, changed into sweats and a T-shirt and laid down on the couch. But he didn't sleep. Rain was beating up on the tin roof. "When it rains it pours," he muttered again to himself. He wasn't even thinking of the weather.

Chapter Two

Dawn was already conducting the choir of birds outside Judge Mullens' bedroom in his clapboard house as he slid as quietly as he could under the blankets. He savored the warmth, the way the soft light of early morning illuminated his wife's face. All these years he tried not to wake her up. All these years she slept lightly waiting for him to come home safe.

"Everything ok?" she murmured.

He put an arm around her and drew her close. "Could have been worse. One critical. No deaths."

"Hmmm," she responded, then turned her head to him. She knew him too well, sensed the teneseness in his prone form. "Something else?"

"You'll never guess who came before me in court last night—Grady Henderson."

"Will's girl? Is she in trouble?"

"She's certainly troubled. She's not handling his passing very well." He ran down the charges, tried to explain what had happened, even though he wasn't entirely clear and the missing details still nagged at him.

"What did you do?"

"Hopefully the right thing," he said. Then he closed his eyes and gave himself over to exhaustion.

Trooper James Oplin was back at the shore of Garnet Lake at dawn. He wore his uniform, but he wasn't on duty, hadn't been for more than 12 hours, but that hadn't gotten him off the Northway any sooner. The bus had been empty except for the driver and two passengers. The truck had been full of Florida oranges on the way to Montreal.

What a mess. Something had crossed the highway in front of them. The two drivers had agreed on that. But what had it been? One swore it was a man. The other claimed it was a small bear or a large dog. Jim had given them both a breathalyzer. They were both sober.

Jim's head pounded. He dabbed a finger carefully underneath his nose. Finally it had stopped bleeding. An EMT at the site of the bus crash had checked him out. Like Jim had already guessed, his nose was broken and there wasn't a damned thing he could do about it. And nothing the EMT gave him had killed the pain.

At least one of his headaches was sitting in a cell in the Warren County Jail waiting for her Stepdaddy to bail her out. He stifled a growl at the mere thought of Grady Henderson. Any expression hurt too much now. All he wanted was to get home and have breakfast and a cup of coffee. No orange juice. He couldn't stand the smell any more, had been fresh-squeezing it all along the Northway in his size twelve boots in the rain. But there was something he needed to confirm before he went home.

He threw his purple-banded hat onto the passenger's seat of his Crown Royal and got out of the car, trying to stay out of the muck and failing despite the fact he had a light step for a brawny guy. He was a good tracker, due more to all the hunting he'd done over the years than any training he'd had in the academy. It took him just a few minutes to find what he'd suspected.

He'd noticed a pattern over the past year: burglaries where nothing valuable was missing. Fires set. Not the kind to destroy, the kind meant to cook food or keep warm. And a larger than average footprint at the scene, a bare foot.

Here it was, turned into a puddle by last night's rain, next to Henderson's dainty prints. He leaned in and picked the heel of her shoe out of the muck and turned it around between his fingers. He looked at the other print. This was evidence that would help her case. But what did he really have? An elusive Bigfoot that he hadn't been able to track down since he first saw signs of him last summer.

Grady Henderson could buy herself out of the charges filed against her. Jim wasn't going to stick his neck out again with some kooky Bigfoot theory. He had been the laughing stock of his troop last summer. With two kids and a wife he wanted to keep, he needed a promotion and he wasn't going to get it by chasing Sasquatch, or at least letting anyone know he was doing it.

He tossed the heel of Grady's shoe deep into the woods and turned to leave, stepping hard on the prints in the muddy ground. The only mark left was from his polished size twelve boots.

Thane woke at dawn without an alarm, which was a good thing since he was down on the couch and the clock was up in the loft next to his bed on which Grady Henderson was sleeping. He rubbed his face with his hands and got up, taking the stairs to the loft quietly. He wasn't into kink; he had never woken up to find a girl handcuffed in his bed, until now. Grady Henderson was still asleep, tangled in his comforter. Her skirt had ridden up her thigh, and his first instinct was to either pull it down, or cover her up, but either might wake her and he didn't want to risk it. Right now, dirty as it was, her face was calm and peaceful, and he knew that would change as soon as she woke up. He stood for a moment longer looking down at her. It was a pretty face, when it wasn't angry, and he wondered if it was only like that when she slept. He turned away and pulled out a pair of old work jeans and a grey T-shirt from his dresser as quietly as he could. Beau had made his way up onto the bed, and Thane whispered his name. "Come on," Thane said softly. Beau looked at him, yawned wide enough to show his pink gums, then put his head back down.

Thane shrugged and turned to the stairs. Beau would be one less thing to worry about then, and Thane had enough worries already.

When Grady awoke, she wasn't sure where she was. Her wrists hurt. Her body ached. She felt like she'd been in a fight. She opened her eyes and remembered she had been. She looked down at her streaked and tattered blouse and skirt and away to the wooden walls. Above the bed was a window like a porthole high up in the gable end of the wall, beyond which was only mist.

She felt like she could be in water, on a ship. Shipwrecked, she thought as another memory flitted before her mind's eye and explained the stiffness in her neck. She reached up with her right hand to rub her eyes which felt filled with grit. Her left hand tagged along and she remembered she was cuffed as she rubbed both eyes with both hands, and couldn't tell if the dirt on them came from her face or had already been there. She pushed against the thick fleecy blankets and jumped out of bed as she realized the blanket was alive. Thane McMaster's dog lifted up its head and stared at her expectantly with a moist open jaw. She thought about trying to make the bed, she could have done it easily enough even with cuffed hands, folding the comforter in two, but she didn't want to get any closer to the dog, and she'd made a mess of the bed anyway, like she knew she would, the dirt and mud from her ruined clothes rubbing onto the white comforter. That's what she'd meant when she'd told Thane McMasters she couldn't sleep there. Why hadn't he given her the couch?

Grady backed away, and made her way gingerly down a narrow staircase with runners of halved logs. It was a small place, but well thought-out. It felt like the inside of a forest. Tongue and groove pine formed a canopy of the cathedral ceiling where rough exposed beams held the house together in a puzzle of joints. She passed the bathroom, the only room with a door, but instead of stepping into the shower, she turned and went in search of Thane's phone, since her cell phone was still in her car over at the lake. Then she did what any good Long Island girl would do in an emergency. Grady called her lawyer.

Fred Morey was an old friend of her father's and Grady had known him since she was a child. His secretary put Grady on hold. She listened to the hum on the line, but in the background she thought she heard another familiar noise. She lifted her eyes from Thane's desk and its neat stack of papers to the window above it and watched the fog drag itself wisp by wisp away from the ground. Except it wasn't ground. Beneath the fog was Garnet Lake. She gasped. That noise she'd been hearing was the slap of the water against the shore.

"What's so important, Grady, that you had to drag me out of a meeting?" Fred Morey said as he came on the phone.

"I need bail money."

"For whom?"

"For me."

"Oh, Grady," his voice sounded tired. "What have you done?"

"Nothing! I came up to stop the renovations on the cabin up here on Garnet Lake. Which by the way is a demolition not a renovation, and I got accused of trying to burn down the outshed on the property."

"Where are you? The Warren County Jail?"

"No, and that's another thing. The local yokel judge up here gave me house arrest, and I'd like you to sue him."

"At the cabin? I don't imagine it's livable."

"No, with some construction worker."

There was a long pause. When Fred spoke again, she thought she heard a smile in his voice. "Well, Justice Mullens must have a good reason for what he did."

"The reason is, he's a nutcase and. . . wait a minute, how do you know his name?"

"We go fishing when I get up to my place in Lake Placid. Which is almost never. Grady, I'm in the middle of a meeting here."

"So you're not going to sue him on my behalf?"

"No, Grady,"

"Well, what are you going to do about the bail money?"

"Did you call your mother?"

"She's on her honeymoon. Not reachable. There's got to be something you can do for me."

"I can let you figure it out for yourself. It's not my job to bail you out, Grady."

"It was your job to set up the trust, and I'm demanding you give me the funds."

"I'm sorry Grady, I can't do anything without Richard Hartwell's direction. I can't do anything about the tenets of the trust, and I certainly can't have funds released directly to you until you're 25."

"That's two more years, I can't wait that long."

"You'll have to."

"Not unless I sue Richard Hartwell."

"Grady, you'll eat up your own money that way."

"Better to waste it than have Hartwell use it to do more damage. You didn't have anything against him tearing the cabin down, did you?"

"It's not my call, Grady, he has the power of Trusteeship, and I assumed they informed you of the plans for the cabin."

"No one tells me anything, that's why I'm going to sue for mismanagement...unless you release the funds to me."

"Grady, it's out of my hands. I can't change the trust. Look I have it right here and it says you have to be 25, or married."

"Married?! No one told me that! How archaic can you be?"

"It's not me, it's what your father wanted."

"And he wanted that?? This is New York state, not Wuthering Heights! That can't possibly be legal."

"Those were his wishes, and we're bound to abide by them."

"Why would he do that to me?"

"Because he loved you. Grady, don't take this the wrong way, but you tend to be impulsive."

"And you know what you are? Fired!"

His chuckle seemed unconcerned. "See? And you can't fire me, I don't work for you exactly."

Grady sighed. "If I'm so impulsive, maybe I'll just marry the next guy I see, just to get at my money. Did he think about that?"

"You don't trust people very easily, Grady. I think your father thought if you did find a man you'd let close enough to marry you, he'd be one damned good man."

For a moment she couldn't say anything.

"Grady, are you still there?"

"Not for long," she said quietly. She heard a truck pull into the drive. "I've got to go."

"What are you going to do?" There was wariness and admonition in Fred's voice.

"Marry the next guy I see. Don't expect an invitation to the wedding. I think we'll elope."

"But Grady you don't know—"

She knew enough. She ended the call to start something that she would probably regret. But she just didn't see another option.

Thane had been out early. Sterling Construction was being paid to bail out a flooded basement in North Creek. It didn't take long, especially with his thoughts on how to get Grady Henderson bailed out and out of his house. He stopped at the Hartwell site on the way back home. Jack Hanson was hard at work. He'd removed his dozer and he was working a small rusty crane with a claw, moving pieces of the broken cabin into a dump truck.

Thane stood for a moment and watched. The guts of the cabin lay strewn around: a broken kitchen chair, a coffee pot, a rain-soaked sleeping bag oozing its stuffing into the mud. He shook his head. Nobody had bothered to clean the cabin out. He was about to turn away when the claw picked up a section of wall. Beneath it was a cardboard box, beat up but dry.

"Hold up, Jack," Thane yelled. Carefully he worked his way to the box, watching Jack out of the corner of his eye, but he didn't have to worry, Hanson was stepping down out of the cab.

"I didn't mean anything by it, I just meant to scare her off. You think they'll arrest me?" Jack said taking off his frayed cap and running it through his hands.

"I don't think so," Thane said.

Jack blew out a breath and put his cap back on.

He probably had nothing to worry about as far as the authorities were concerned, but Grady Henderson? Thane didn't think she was through with Jack Hanson, especially if she saw the cabin now, or what was left of it.

Jack got back into the cab and Thane didn't say anything more. He hefted the exposed carton and threw it into the bed of his truck. Then he collected Grady's belongings from her car. There wasn't much there, just a purse and an overnight bag and a backpack.

After a quick stop at the State Trooper station in town, where luckily Jim Oplin was not on duty, he was back at the cabin with a key to unlock Grady Henderson's unfashionable bracelets.

When he opened the door to the cabin (it was never locked), he saw her standing at his desk, tapping her finger absent-mindedly against his private papers. She glanced over at him. She was in the same tattered state as yesterday, barefoot, her makeup smeared, her hair unbrushed. He approached her warily, the way he would something wild, but in need of help. It was never a safe thing to do.

"I found this stuff in your car, thought you might want it." He placed the bags at her feet without taking his eyes off her.

She nodded, but didn't even thank him. Her fingers were still tapping at the desk and he lifted her hands to find the lock on the cuffs.

"Could I ask you something?" she said.

Thane nodded as he concentrated on angling her wrists towards him.

"Would you marry me?"

Thane almost dropped the key. "Are you—?" He stopped himself before he said something he'd regret, but she finished the sentence for him.

"Am I crazy? Is that what you wanted to say? No. I'm not crazy. I'm rich. Or I will be," she said in a voice that was quiet, but bitter. "I have a trust that says I can't get access to my money until I'm 25, or married."

"And you want to marry me?"

"Right now you've got the most vested in this relationship, the quicker I get to my trust, the quicker I can post bail, and the sooner I'm gone."

"So to get rid of you, I should marry you?"

"Don't worry, I'd pay you. I need the ring, you need the money. A match made in heaven."

"Who says I need money?" he said slowly.

She nodded at the desk. "The promissory notes you signed with Sterling Construction. They owe you $50,000 and it looks like you're drawing on your 401K because of it."

"You've been looking through my private things?"

"They're lying here for anyone to see."

"Because no one is supposed to be here!"

"You don't want me here and I don't want to be here. Look, we can help each other. Consider it a simple business transaction. I'll give you $25,000 as soon as I get access to my money, so I can make bail and you'll get another $25,000 as soon as we divorce."

"No,"

She blew out a breath. "Fine, $30,000."

He squeezed her wrist harder than he meant to and she flinched as he unlocked the cuffs. "You can't buy me."

"Anyone and everyone has their price."

"I'm not just anyone."

She looked at him and he met her stare. Her eyes narrowed as if she were noticing him for the first time. He didn't blink and after a long moment she looked away. He didn't know if it was by accident that her eyes dropped to his financial papers.

"So, I'm assuming your answer is a no," she said, but it sounded like a question that hung there between them as she rubbed her freed wrists. "I'm going to get cleaned up," she said, picking up her duffel bag. "Who knows how long I'll be staying," she said as she turned.

He flipped his papers over, then caught her briefly by the upper arm before she could walk away. "For future reference, my business is my business."

She acted like she hadn't heard. Thane stared after her for a moment before he stalked from the cabin and slammed the door shut behind him. Who was he kidding? She was already in his business and he was already mixed up in hers.

Thane didn't get very far. On his back deck he almost knocked down his neighbor.

"What is it, Dan, I'm busy," he said, more gruffly than he'd meant.

"Can't afford the time for an old man, huh?"

"There's a lot I can't afford right now," Thane said.

"What's that?" Dan Hardin put a large weathered hand to his ear.

"Nothing. Just tell me what you need."

"Your ladder. Didn't want to borrow it without asking."

"Never stopped you before," Thane muttered under his breath.

"Won't stop me from giving you a shiner," the old man squared his broad stooped shoulders. "It'll match your lip. What kind of trouble you get yourself into last night?"

Thane didn't want to go into it. He put a placating hand on the old man's back. "It's nothing. Come on, I'll get that ladder."

He led the way up the steep stony path across the road to his barn and pushed open the wide door on rollers. While he picked the extension ladder off its hooks, Dan poked his cane at the custom furniture off to the side. "Ya ain't sold none of this yet?"

"I've had some interest in them."

"Interest ain't worth a pisshole in the snow. What you need is cash. Upfront. Can't pay your taxes with interest."

Thane swallowed a reply as he hefted the ladder onto his shoulder. His town and county taxes were four months overdue. The assessments had doubled over last year's because he lived on lake-front property. He owned two acres. 10 feet of which technically touched the water, wedged between swamp on one side and state land on the other.

He led the way just a few hundred yards up the dirt road to Dan's simple farmhouse, with a porch that warped more than it wrapped around.

"What were you planning on doing with this ladder anyway?" Thane asked.

"Just replacing that piece of roofing."

Dan used his cane as a pointer to show Thane a 5-foot section of metal lying on the ground. There was no way the old man could handle that. Thane swore under his breath. He set the ladder up against the house and hefted the tin. Once he got it up there, he wasn't sure where to tack it in; the plywood of the roof underneath was spongy in spots.

"You know what you need?" Dan asked. "You need a wife. A real one. Not a fancy like you brought up here."

"You mean fiancée," Thane corrected him.

"I say what I mean, and I mean fancy. I seen those shoes she wore! You wouldn't need spikes like that unless you were hiking Crane Mountain in the dead of winter."

Thane sighed. He'd used half his savings to buy the dilapidated shack on the shore of Garnet Lake. He'd spent the other half renovating it himself on weekends with help from Cal, before quitting his job in an architectural firm to move up full-time and finish the work. He'd had it all planned out. The old barn on the property was the perfect workshop to build his rustic furniture in that he could then sell.

But a plan is a flimsy thing, and there was so much it didn't include, like the septic system not passing inspection. A modern engineered system cost him 10 grand. Then the Adirondack Park Agency told him his roof ridge exceeded height restrictions for lake front. He'd either have to make it lower (tear the roof down) or pay a hefty fine. He'd designed it himself, he knew it was just right, but it had cost him thousands in legal fees for them to see it his way.

And Bridget, his fiancée? She was in consulting, which meant she could work from anywhere. After a couple of months in Garnet Lake she decided she really preferred to work from Manhattan.

A year ago he'd had everything, a promising career, a beautiful fiancée, and he'd given it all up for a dream of getting back to Garnet Lake. Now at 27, he was struggling to hold onto his house—the only thing he had left. He was working so hard, he had no more time to build furniture, let alone do the things that had drawn him back here, like fishing and hiking. When he wasn't working for Cal, he was doing favors like this for his crotchety neighbor who never paid him, not even with a thank you.

Dan was still talking. "See, if you'd put a ring on her finger, it wouldn't have been so easy for her to just up and leave at the first dusting of snow. I'd like to see you get married proper before I quit sucking air."

"You might get your wish sooner than you think," Thane mumbled.

"What's that?"

Thane glanced down at Dan. His black horn rims reflected the sun, or was that a glint in his eyes? Thane had long ago suspected the old bastard wasn't hard of hearing at all.

Things looked different for Grady after she'd showered and changed into her jeans and V-neck cotton t-shirt that had been in her overnight bag. Things looked worse. She didn't bother putting on the sneakers that were in the bottom of her bag. She pulled Thane's flannel jacket from its wooden peg and slipped out the only entrance on the side onto his deck, that wrapped around to face the lake. She breathed in the sweet scent of pine under the dappled sky.

She hadn't really noticed the outside of Thane's cabin last night. She'd been almost in a trance, but that wasn't the only reason. The board and batten siding didn't stand out. It was plain compared to the intricate beauty of the inside, almost like Thane chose to camouflage it. Her father's cabin was almost directly across the lake, protected from sight by a jag in the shoreline. The view she'd always enjoyed had been inverted. She glanced behind her, saw the way the land leveled off to the right but tilted sharply up to the left behind Thane's barn. She knew that was the beginning of Ethan Ridge, even though from this close she couldn't see straight to the top like she could from the other side of the lake. Her perspective had changed. In so many ways.

The bulkhead was like the rim of a cup that had been filled too high from last night's rain. She walked to the edge of the aluminum dock and sat down. It had soaked in the spring sun, but when she dipped her feet into the clear water, she couldn't tell if she had put them into fire or ice; it felt the same as the rage inside her. It had turned to a cold blank space.

There wasn't anything she could do about her father's cabin. Just like nothing was ever going to bring her father back. She could sue Richard Hartwell, but she had no money. Could she file a lien against the Sterling company and stop any planned construction? She wasn't exactly sure what that entailed, but any kind of messy legal proceeding would buy her time to save at least the remnants of the cabin. She had to do something.

She had to get out of here. But she realized suddenly that last thought felt like a lie against the honest clarity of this setting. She wanted to stay in this moment forever, with the green absolutes of the trees, the true blueness of the sky. Across the ageless water was her father's cabin, and if she tried, she could make herself believe it was still standing.

A splash next to her shocked her out of her thoughts. As she watched the ripples throw themselves against the bulkhead, she saw a flat rock skim once, twice, again, and then again over the silvery surface of Garnet Lake. She turned her head and stared at the bizarre figure who stared back at her behind black horn-rimmed glasses. His slight figure was buried in grey coveralls. Rubber boots swallowed his legs almost to the knees.

"Lookin' to catch yourself a fish, or pneumonia?" the old man's voice was gruff, and it warred with the broad smile on his wizened face. He approached her slowly and held out a bear-sized hand, rough and calloused. Grady took it.

"Well?" he asked as he yanked her to her feet with more strength than she'd thought possible. "Is Thane going to make an honest woman of you?"

"No," she said and was struck by the way the old man's face fell. "I'm way too honest already."

Dan had tired of supervising Thane, or rather haranguing him and had disappeared. After Thane finished patching Dan's roof, he put away his own ladder in the barn up the hill from his house. He had forgotten about the box he'd found at the Henderson's cabin on Garnet Lake under the rubble and he threw it into the barn just in case it rained again.

When he came out of the barn he spotted Dan Hardin at the water's edge below the cabin. For a moment he wondered who Dan was talking to. He paused when he realized with a shock it was Grady

Henderson. He didn't recognize her. Close-fitting jeans were rolled up to her calves. Her hair was pulled back into a carefree ponytail, she was wearing a flannel jacket—his jacket—but the reason he hadn't recognized her? She was laughing.

She heard him coming and turned her face to him, and for a moment her eyes were bright and happy, her mouth open, her expression curious and welcoming. Then she realized it was him and the light in her eyes went out like a snuffed candle.

Dan poked him not very gently with his cane. "Whatcha keepin' a pretty girl like this a secret for?"

"It's not a secret, Dan. She's just…just living here for a short time, until…" Until she made bail? Until this whole story got straightened out, about who set fire to the contents of the storage shed at the Hartwell place.

"Until what? 'Til we're all resting in peace?"

"I'm waiting for you to leave me in peace," Thane said.

"You'll be waiting a long time for that," the old man chuckled. But he took the hint and he shuffled off up the hill, tipping his overlarge cap to Grady.

She watched him with a smile and then turned back to Thane and the smile disappeared.

"Would you mind taking me to the Clerk's office in town?" she asked in a clipped voice.

"I never agreed to…to your proposition."

She flinched at the word.

"I know. Which is why I can't get at my money. If I could, I'd sue Richard Hartwell for mismanagement and hire your Sterling Construction to rebuild the cabin. My only option now is to file a lien on the cabin and stop construction entirely," she said.

"You can't do that!"

"I can try. But since I don't have a driver's license I need you to drive me into town."

"You think I'll drive you into town to help you put a lien on my friend's company, which could put him out of business?"

"Fine, I'm sure Mr. Hardin would be more than happy to take

me."

"No!" Thane said automatically. "He shouldn't be driving, but he's too damned stubborn to admit it. Promise me you won't ask him."

She shrugged. "Take me to town, and I'll promise."

Thane gritted his teeth and looked down at her bare feet. "Get your shoes, then get in the truck," he said tightly.

For once he didn't have to nag Beau to hurry. The old dog seemed to have the energy of a puppy as he scrambled into the cab over Grady. Thane drove extra slowly over the ruts in the gravel road. The Ranger could take it, but Thane needed time to think. He had to come up with some way to get a handle on a situation that was pulling him in deeper and deeper.

The town clerk, Gladys, according to the nameplate on the desk, looked up as Grady and Thane entered her office at the municipal center in Garnet Lake. She greeted Thane by name and then turned to Grady expectantly as if waiting to be introduced. Her glasses swayed around her neck suspended from a jeweled chain.

"I'd like to apply for a—" Grady never completed the word lien, because Thane interrupted her.

"A marriage license, Gladys."

"You said you wouldn't marry me," Grady looked at him in surprise.

"I don't recall actually giving you an answer" he said.

"You said you couldn't be bought."

"This isn't about the money," Thane said curtly. "I can't let you ruin Cal's company."

"I'm not out to ruin anybody."

"What are you out for then?"

Grady looked at him for as long as she could stand the intensity in his brown eyes, then she looked away, focusing instead on the pocked wooden counter, running her finger over the worn surface.

"I don't know," she said in a tired voice. There was silence except the nervous rattling of the clerk's glasses. The woman pushed an application for a marriage license tentatively across the counter until it touched Grady's finger.

"Do you want this or not, honey?" she asked.

Grady didn't answer, she just picked up a pen and began filling in the blanks, if only to have something to do.

"Is the second M in McMasters capital or lower case?" she asked absently, glancing up and catching the bewildered glance of the clerk. Grady sighed and pushed the form in Thane's direction and kept her eyes glued on the ghostly imprints of past signatures that had bled into the countertop.

The clerk took the paper Thane handed her and looked it over. "Okay, we'll see you after 24 hours when the waiting period is up," she said.

"24 hours?" Grady looked up. "I can't wait that long!"

The clerk patted her on the forearm. "I know it's hard to wait, honey, but believe me," she leaned in conspiratorially. "It's worth it."

Then in a more business-like tone, she said: "Oh, and I'll need to see your I.D.s. Do you have your driver's license?"

"Ask the judge," Grady responded sullenly.

"Ask me what?" Judge Mullens' gruff tone made Grady jump, and she turned to see him standing in the open doorway. He didn't wait for an answer, but walked over to the counter and took the paper from the clerk's hand, glanced at it and grunted.

"Come with me," he demanded, as he disappeared into his chambers through the adjoining door. Thane followed. Grady paused a moment before she too entered the small office, crowned by a metal desk overflowing with files and loose papers. The chair squeaked as the judge dropped into it. He lifted his reading glasses from a pile and began studying the paper in his hands.

"So," he said slowly. "You want to get married. That was quick."

"Today, if possible," she said.

He looked up over his half-lenses. He didn't say anything, but his eyebrows drove themselves deeper into the furrows in his forehead.

"There's a waiting period, you know," he said.

Grady shrugged. "I also know you don't exactly do things by the book around here, I'm just asking that you speed up the process."

"Why?" he asked bluntly.

"I have to be 25, or married to come into my trust."

"You're not very patient, are you?" The corner of his mouth twitched as his eyes dropped again to the paper. "So, you're willing to rush headlong into a partnership with someone you don't even know. Marriage is a serious endeavor," he said solemnly. "Have you thought about this? I mean really thought about it? You're sure you want to go through with this?"

"Positive!" Grady responded.

He looked up and a slow smile spread from his lips to his eyes. "I was talking to Thane."

He glanced at Thane now. So did Grady. She saw the tenseness in his jaw as he stood there silently, like a man condemned for a crime he didn't commit. She waited for him to say something, but the door crashing open drowned out any answer he would have given.

Jim Oplin's frame filled the doorway, blocking the fluorescent light from the clerk's office and making the room seem as dark as his expression.

"Opie." The judge said calmly. "You need something?"

"I need to know," the state trooper began in a voice that was artificially calm, and still threatening, despite the twang caused by his swollen nose. "Why she isn't in the Warren County Jail." He jerked a thumb towards Grady.

"Because we didn't have the manpower to get her there, and I'm not satisfied with the whole story. And because I used my discretion."

"You think she's innocent?" Oplin asked, his voice incredulous.

"I don't know what to think," the judge said simply, tossing the marriage application onto his desk.

"What's going on here?" Oplin asked as he glanced at it. His eyes grew wide as he reached out to pick it up. "Is this a joke?"

"Not at all," the judge said. "I was just explaining to these two before me that marriage is a serious endeavor. I'm glad you're here. We needed another witness." The judge got up and took a step toward the open door. "Gladys, could you come in here, please?"

Oplin moved slack-jawed out of the way to make room for the slight woman.

The judge looked at him hard. "Since you have no reservations, let's get started."

He instructed Thane to take Grady's hands in his, which he did after a long moment's hesitation. He held hers gently, but firmly, and as the full realization hit her of what she was about to do, she found herself holding on to him tighter than necessary.

"You could at least look at each other," the judge said with a sigh.

She looked up then into Thane's brown eyes, serious and guarded. His jaw was clenched. She was making a mistake, and making a mistake for him too, but damn it, that was the only thing she was good at lately.

She had never really imagined herself getting married. That would have involved trusting someone. And she certainly hadn't imagined it like this. But it was just as well. She had no father to walk her down the aisle anyway, so who cared if this wasn't a fairytale wedding? But something in her knew it was wrong, and sent water into her eyes to sabotage her. She looked down again. Damn the judge.

The ceremony couldn't last much longer, or could it? The judge cleared his throat, then rambled through a scripture reading.

"I think we can skip the sermon," Grady said sullenly when he was finished.

"I think this situation especially calls for a lesson," he said. "Marriage is a partnership. If it were a business it would be a limited liability company. You've entered into this arrangement for richer or poorer. Outside influences might make you destitute, or you could win the lottery. What's important is what happens within the marriage. Never leave your spouse poorer. Enrich one another. Bring all your assets to this partnership, your compassion, your strengths, and you'll be stronger, tougher, together than you could ever be alone."

Grady blinked a few times. She moved her gaze from Thane's strong hands that would never willingly give—at least to her, and stared at a pull in the beige carpet, trying hard to think about anything but words that were meant for her ears, but would never fit her situation.

"You may now exchange rings. If you have any."

Out of the corner of her eye, Grady saw the Justice struggling to remove his own ring. He got it off with a grunt and handed it to Grady. "This is only a loan. Gladys, where's that lost and found box?"

While the judge rifled through the cardboard box full of discarded scarves and books and glasses, she slipped the ring over Thane's finger. It was loose, but would probably not get lost, she hoped. She didn't look at Thane, she couldn't. Instead she watched the judge pick up and hold a simple silver band up to the light. He was squinting at the tiny red stone in the setting.

"Looks like a garnet," he said as he handed it to Thane. Grady watched as Thane slipped it onto her finger. It fit perfectly.

"I now pronounce you man and wife," the Justice said. "I'm guessing you'd rather skip the 'kiss the bride' part," he added, glancing pointedly at Thane's split lip.

There was no music, no congratulations, only the slamming of the door as Oplin stormed out of the small room.

The justice resumed his seat and stared over his glasses at Thane and Grady with a sardonic smile. "Now if you don't mind Mr. and Mrs. McMasters, I have work to do. I wish you many happy years together."

And with that, Thane, Grady's husband, opened the door for her and they stepped over the threshold.

Grady stood with Thane on the steps of the municipal building. Neither of them spoke for a little while. They both studied the small supermarket across the street.

"I'll walk up to the bank," Grady finally broke the silence. "I'll open up an account and get the transfer started. We'll make this as quick and painless as possible."

From the corner of her eye she noticed him reflexively bring a hand up and run a finger gingerly along his swollen lip.

"I'm sorry," she said.

Thane dropped his hand and shrugged. "Nothing that can't be undone with some paperwork, I guess."

"No, I meant about your lip. I'm sorry. I don't remember doing it."

"You're sorry you did it, or you're sorry you don't remember doing it?"

She didn't know him well enough to know if the side of his mouth that wasn't swollen lifted up in a grim smile or a teasing one.

"You know what I mean." Grady said.

"Did you mean it when you said you wouldn't put a lien on Sterling construction?"

"I told you that already. Doesn't my word stand for anything?"

"Up here it's everything." He put out his hand. "Promise me?"

She put her hand in his for the second time today. "Yes. I promise."

Still she felt him searching her eyes, gauging her sincerity. His scrutiny was too intense, reminding her of the promise she'd made only minutes ago to love, honor and cherish 'til death do them part, and how she had no intention of keeping that.

"Let me go," she said easing her hand out of his firm grip. "So I can get to the bank. The sooner I'm out of here, the better for everyone," she said.

He let her go, and again she had that feeling of drifting. And she wondered if what she'd just said had been a lie? Would it really be better for her to leave here?

Thane watched Grady walk away. Would she keep her promise and not put a lien on Sterling Construction? Part of him knew she would. The other part of him said he didn't know her at all, how could he be so sure. Lost in thought he went to his pickup and climbed in. He didn't start the engine. He couldn't have driven away, not with the thick forearm laying across his open window. He looked up at the rest of the 6' 4" body attached to it, and into the very angry face of his best friend who was asking him exactly what kind of a mess he'd gotten them both into. Except it took Jim Oplin a whole lot of words to say all that, because more than half of them were curses.

"Me?" asked Thane. "you took it to a whole new level."

"When you called me from the work site, you said you were scared."

"I said 'just scare her off.'"

"Scare her off? You said she was going to blow something up."

"Geez, Opie, I said 'I didn't want this thing blowing up.'" Thane shook his head. "Her stepfather is basically the only paying client Cal has."

"I don't care who her daddy is. She's a nutcase."

He went on to question Thane's decision to marry Grady and his sanity in so many words, again most of them expletives.

Thane interrupted him. "She was going to put a lien against Cal's company. You know I can't let that happen. He'd lose everything. And you know I stand to lose if he does."

"So you married her? What sense does that make? How the hell is that going to save your money?"

"If she marries or turns 25, she comes into her trust fund. She'll make bail and be out of here. And leave Cal alone."

"And you believe her." Opie snorted then winced immediately in pain.

Thane looked away from his friend's bruised nose and stared out the windshield.

"You've seen this trust? Got the papers?" Opie pressed. "So if she even gets this money, then what? You get a divorce and go your merry ways. You think you can just snap your fingers and end it? First you have to file a separation agreement, then you have to wait a year. And what if she won't sign?" He went into another tirade.

Thane didn't want to hear it. He was already questioning his own judgment. It had all happened so fast. He'd thought he could buy some time by agreeing to Grady's proposal, he'd have had at least 24 hours to get out of it. But Judge Mullens had waived the waiting period.

"Are you done?" Thane asked tightly.

"I am. But let me tell you, buddy, you're just gettin' started." Jim shook his head, pushed himself away and slapped his hand on the hood of the pickup. Before he turned his back on Thane, he muttered one last sentence full of curses, the gist of which was: Thane may never get rid of this Grady Henderson.

Chapter Three

At the bank Grady didn't have a chance to sit and wait for the manager, Robert Gould. He overheard her giving her name to the teller behind the thin glass at the counter.

"Well, well, Grady Henderson!" he said covering her hand in his and pumping it up and down like he was drawing water out of a well. He didn't let go until he had steered her into his office and pushed her gently into an over-large leather chair.

"What brings you to the lollipop store?" he asked with a wide smile. "Remember that's what you used to call us?" He pushed a bowl of colorful pops in her direction. "Here you go! For old time's sake!"

Grady declined. "What I'd really like is to open an account."

"Well we'd be happy to have you. I just need some I.D. and your social security number."

He turned to the computer that looked new and out of place on his antique desk cluttered with family pictures. Grady noticed how nothing had changed here except that monitor. The chocolate paneling on the wall buckled a little behind the faded pictures of waterfalls and forests.

"Um. I haven't got my license on me. . . at the moment."

Robert waved his hand in the air like he was swatting an imaginary fly. "That's all right. I've known you since you were a baby. In fact ..." he swiveled back towards her. "I remember the first time your Dad brought you into the lollipop store. Gosh he was so proud." He looked down at his hands. "I'm really sorry, Grady, about what happened to him."

After seven months she still never knew what to say. Why did people always apologize?

"It wasn't your fault," she said trying to let a note of humor creep into her voice, but it wouldn't come.

He smiled for a second but it didn't reach his eyes which Grady noticed for the first time seemed milkier behind his thick rimless glasses. His hair she saw now had retreated farther from his forehead since she'd last seen him. "Don't you wish it could be though?" he said.

"Excuse me?" Grady didn't follow him.

"Don't you wish it could be someone's fault?" he said. "It would make things easier somehow, wouldn't it, to have somebody to blame?"

Grady remembered now he'd lost his wife a year or two back.

"I'm sorry about Mrs. Gould," Grady said hesitantly, using the same awkward helpless phrase.

He made the waving motion again. "Life goes on," he said but there was a tiredness in his voice that told her it didn't go on as it used to, that his life walked with a definite limp.

He turned back to the computer, his back hunched like he had to protect the keyboard, as he began typing in her information. He pecked at the keys one by one with a stiff pointer finger. But pecking had to do with hungry birds and she wished this bird was a little hungrier.

"Would you mind if I use your phone?" she asked, and he nodded without looking up.

Impulsively, she dialed the insurance company where she worked as a web designer in a grey little cubicle in a grey building, staring at a grey computer screen. Her boss was out.

Grady left a message, short and to the point. "I quit."

She noticed Robert raise his eyebrows, but he didn't say anything.

Then she called her attorney. It took a few minutes for Fred Morey to come on the line.

"Hold on a second," she said instead of a greeting. "Mr. Gould, do you have an account number already that you could give me?"

From the phone she heard Fred's voice. "Account number? What do you need an account number for?"

"So you can transfer my funds from the trust like we talked about this morning."

"I told you Grady you have to be 25."

"Or married. I'll get you a copy of the marriage certificate while you make the transfer." She put a hand over the receiver and spoke to

Robert. "Can you scan something for me?"

He looked at her. "You mean read something for you?"

"Never mind. Do you have a fax machine?"

"Geez, Grady, what have you done now?" Fred said through the phone.

"The only thing I could do. When can I get those funds?" Grady asked.

Fred sighed. "I'll start the paperwork in 30 days."

"30 days?"

"There's a waiting period."

"Why would there be a waiting period?"

"To keep you from making a stupid decision."

"Why didn't you tell me?"

"I tried. You hung up on me before I could finish."

"What am I going to do now?"

"You're a big girl. I guess you'll figure it out. I'll talk to you in a month."

"Wait!" Grady said quickly. "I need bail money. You can't just leave me stranded here. My Dad was your best customer. He was your friend ..."

Grady let the words hang there until the silence became uncomfortable. Finally Fred sighed "How much do you need?"

"50,000."

Another sigh. "I'll see if I can get an advance, or I'll make you a loan. Just give me the account info. And Grady,"

"I know, stay out of trouble."

"What do you think your Dad would say about all this?"

Grady didn't respond. Instead she recited numbly the account number that Robert had scrawled on a ledger and pushed shyly across the desk at her. Grady hung up on Fred without saying goodbye and stared at the phone. Robert shifted uncomfortably in his chair, but Grady barely noticed. Of course her Dad wouldn't have approved, but damn it, he wasn't around to give his consent.

Robert's voice interrupted her musings. "I'll be with you in just a minute, Cal," he said looking around her. Her head snapped around so she could see the lanky form in jeans, boots and a work-stained T-Shirt leaning in the doorway.

"You're Cal Sterling?" she asked.

"Yes Ma'am," he answered, pulling a ragged blue baseball cap off of his blond curls and giving a bow. "And you are?"

"Your new partner, or the person who will put you out of business, it's up to you."

Cal Sterling took a step backwards. Grady got up and followed him. They stood halfway between the teller's counter and Robert's office.

Cal's flirty expression had disappeared. "You're the Henderson girl, aren't you?"

"And you were responsible for taking my cabin down."

Cal put up both hands as if she held a gun. "Just taking orders."

"From Richard Hartwell," she said. "And what's your next order?"

"I really can't discuss it with you."

"Well maybe we can discuss me putting a lien against Sterling Construction for what you did without my permission. That cabin is. . . was in trust for me." She had promised Thane she wouldn't do it, but Cal didn't need to know that just yet.

"Listen, I don't want to get involved in your family issues," Cal said.

"It's too late. You already are. Do you have a contract with Richard Hartwell?"

"Yes ... and no. Well, not signed anyway. He's approved the designs."

"For what?"

"A house."

"How big?"

"3,000 square feet."

"The cabin wasn't even 500. The Park Agency would never approve that."

"You'd be surprised. We're waiting on approval and the permit."

"If you built on the exact same footprint, the exact dimensions as the cabin, would you need a permit?"

He shook his head. "Just from the town and county."

Grady took a step back into the bank manager's office and pulled a piece of paper from the printer without asking and used the door jamb as a blotter and wrote quickly. Impulsive, her father's attorney had called her. She was doing her best to live up to her reputation. She drew two lines at the bottom, signed her name on one and then handed the page to Cal Sterling.

"What's this?" he asked warily. "A lien needs to be more official than that."

"It's a contract for you to do nothing. I don't want you to touch a thing on that property. I need some time to think. I want to know for sure the cabin's beyond repair."

He swallowed hard. "Well if it wasn't beyond repair before, it is now."

"Well, I'm thinking of rebuilding with whatever you could salvage. I'll give you $25,000 as a down payment today. If I decide to rebuild, I'll give you the rest in 30 days when I come into my trust. I don't care what it costs."

He looked for a long moment at the scrawled contract Grady had handed him, and when he glanced up again his eyes were narrowed.

"I'd get a lot more to build that place for Hartwell. And I really don't want to get in the middle of a family feud," he said slowly. She could tell he didn't give a damn about her family relations.

"You know as well as I do, it could take a year to get agency approval on what Hartwell plans. And if he does get approval, I'll sue him and you'll never see your money."

She waited. He would sign. She knew he would. She would give him as much time as he needed. The question was, how much time did she have? From Robert's window she saw Thane McMasters pull his Ranger into the bank parking lot.

"And you don't think Hartwell is going to come down on me?" Cal was saying. "The down payment would have to be more substantial than this if there's going to be bad feelings."

She watched Thane get out of the truck. "All I can get now is $50,000." She said irritably.

"I'll take it," Cal said with a wide grin. He scrawled an amount on the paper, attached a signature that was really just a wavy line, folded the paper and put it in his back pocket. He nodded at the bank manager. "Robert's got my account number. Pleasure doing business with you."

Thane didn't know Grady Henderson long enough to be suspicious about her expressions, but something struck him as she rushed out of the bank to meet him. Her face was flushed. He had noticed Cal's pickup in the lot. Had they had a run in? But they didn't even know each other. And Thane wasn't interested in introducing them right now.

"Everything in order?" he asked. He thought it was odd that she dropped her eyes when she responded.

"Yes. No." She corrected herself and made a nervous motion of tucking a loose strand of her dark hair behind her ear.

"When can you get the bail money?" he asked.

"Well, there's a bit of a complication."

"So you were wrong about the trust." Opie had been right, damn it.

"No! That part's right, it's just there's a waiting period."

"How long?"

"30 days."

A month. Thane removed his cap, ran the ball of his fist over his short-cropped hair and put the hat back on in one motion. He'd been optimistic in having her out of here in a week, hoping it would all be blown over before his parents worked their way back here from Florida in a little less than a month.

Grady looked at him for the first time since exiting the bank. "I'm really sorry."

When he didn't respond, she glanced away, her eyes flicking

44

across the street. There wasn't much to look at, just the small grey stone church, an even smaller white clapboard post office and the old-fashioned movie theater. The marquee still listed the block blusters from two years ago. He wondered if they'd ever open again. Next door was a renovated two-story brick building where the sign read 'Silver and Associates.'

"Is he a good attorney?" Grady asked.

"He's the only attorney."

"If it would make you feel better, we can have him draw up the divorce papers. You know, just to have them ready," she said.

Thane shrugged. "If you'd like."

They began walking. What a strange two days it had been. At least it couldn't get more bizarre. Thane glanced back towards the bank. He swore he saw Cal's blond head for a split second before it ducked beneath the window. Maybe he was wrong.

Maybe things could get more complicated.

John Silver had no associates, and no secretary either. He was young, and seemed to wear his wireless glasses less for his vision than to make himself look older.

He sat across the clear glass table top from Grady and Thane and folded his hands like a priest. "So what brings you here?"

"It's complicated," she said.

"It usually is."

Grady went through as best she could the happenings of the day before, finding out Richard Hartwell had ordered the demolition of her father's cabin. How she had showed up trying to stop it. The dozer driver almost running her down. Her surprise when the trooper came after her. The shed burning.

"I don't remember giving Thane that fat lip and I don't know how the trooper got the broken nose. It's like some of the pieces are missing."

"Were you under the influence of drugs or alcohol?"

"No! I'm not like that. I can prove it. I was stopped twice for speeding on the way up. They would have tested me if they'd thought I was high or whatever."

"How fast were you going?"

Grady fished in her purse for the tickets and pushed them across the desk. His eyebrows went up, high, before he composed his face again and looked up. He put them off to the side.

"We'd better take care of these too, at least try to reduce the points so you don't lose your license," he said.

"I already have. Judge Mullens took my license and remanded me to Thane's care. Which by the way I told him I'd sue him for."

John Silver smiled. "You couldn't get anyone within a 200-mile radius to do that."

"Because he's a good old boy," Grady said.

"Because he's a good guy. There's a difference. He's a bit unorthodox, but he's fair. And besides I think you're in enough legal trouble already. I'll get a copy of the charges against you, and we'll see what we can do. Is there anything else?"

"A few things actually. We need to file for divorce," she said.

Again his eyebrows went up. "Divorce? I didn't think you two knew each other before yesterday. How long have you been married?"

"About an hour," Grady said in a small voice. "I have a trust, which Richard Hartwell manages, or rather mismanages. My goal is to get control of my trust as soon as possible to get it out of his hands and have nothing more to do with them. . .I mean him. To come into my trust I have to be 25. . . or married."

He nodded. "A bit archaic," he said slowly. "But as long as the wishes of the originator aren't illegal, it's perfectly acceptable." He tapped his fingers together lightly. "But why divorce so soon?"

"I thought if we could at least get the paperwork prepared and ready, it would be simpler."

"And on another matter, I'd like to press charges against that dozer operator. If Thane hadn't pushed me out of the way, I'd be dead now."

"Who's the dozer driver?"

"Jack, or Jake Hanson."

Silver glanced quickly at Thane and pursed his lips. "Why don't you take some time to think about it?"

"I don't want to take the time. In 30 days I'll have all the money I need and I'll find someone else to sue him if you won't."

Silver shrugged his shoulders amiably and stood up, extending a hand to each of them. "Then take 30 days to think about it. We'll talk then." He rummaged through a stack of envelopes in his outbox. "Thane, would you mind saving me a stamp and delivering this on your way home, it's pretty urgent," he said.

Something about the look he gave Thane bothered her. As did the look on Thane's face as he took the envelope, glanced at it and the corners of his mouth went down. Thane didn't say anything. In fact he hadn't spoken since greeting the attorney. He gave a curt nod and tucked the manila envelope under his arm. As he turned towards the door, she noticed there was already postage on the envelope.

She was about to follow Thane out the door, but she let it close behind him as Silver called her back.

"What grounds would you give for divorce? Irreconcilable differences? Infidelity? Abuse?" Silver listed them like they were flavors of ice cream.

Grady thought for a moment. "We don't know each other long enough to know if we have irreconcilable differences, but I'd feel wrong about picking the other ones."

"Grady, New York is an equitable state, that means marital assets are distributed fairly not equally. Your inheritance should be considered separate and would be protected in a divorce, but you may be liable for maintenance."

"You mean alimony?" Grady shrugged. "Thane would be welcome to it. But I don't think he'd insist on taking it."

John smiled broadly. "I think you know each other better than you think you do."

Thane's pickup stopped in front of a beaten-up old house. Tarpaper siding was peeling away from the walls. Old machinery littered the front yard, parts lying like forgotten sculptures in the grass.

She turned to see Thane staring at her expectantly as he killed the truck's engine.

"I'll just wait for you here," she said.

She saw his jaw tighten, as he took a deep breath through his nose. "I'd like you to come in with me," he said.

"I'd really rather not."

"Please," he said.

She sighed. "OK."

She tried to open the door, but the latch was stuck. Thane came around to her side and let her out.

"Not you, buddy, too many wires," he said as he pushed Beau back in and closed the door gently.

He stood for a moment looking at the house and then squared his shoulders.

"What's the matter?" Grady asked.

Thane tilted his head towards her and a gave a brief shake of his head. "Let's get this over with," he muttered.

The first thing Grady noticed when she entered the door Thane held open for her was the smell of sickness, that slightly sweet, dankness that would never leave a room no matter how many windows were left open. The second thing was the oxygen tanks. She tried to ignore them and concentrate on the small woman attached to them by the clear plastic tubing underneath her nostrils.

"How are you, Evelyn?" Thane said as he held out his hand to her.

"Fine, just fine," she said, though it was obviously a lie. She only let go of his hand after a long moment to reach for Grady's. Grady was surprised at the strength in it and the sparkle in the bright eyes that were brimming with curiosity.

"Who do you have with you, Thane?" Evelyn asked.

"This is Grady Henderson," he said.

"Any relation to the Hendersons from Pilot Point?"

Grady wrenched her hand away.

"Distantly," she murmured, not wanting to get into anything personal, or painful. Her father couldn't get any more distant than he was now. She rubbed her forehead and tried to keep her eyes off the oxygen tanks.

"I didn't know you had someone in your life," Evelyn said in a rumbly voice.

"Neither did I," Thane said as he handed her the envelope he'd brought. "John Silver asked me to drop this off. He said it was urgent."

She laughed and then coughed. "Hopefully not that urgent," she said as she wriggled a finger under the envelope and ripped it open.

"Why don't you sit a while?" she asked, pulling a stack of magazines from the couch next to her easy chair.

All Grady wanted to do was get away from there, away from those tanks. She felt like she was going to be sick. She put a hand on her stomach.

"I'm really sorry," Grady said. "I'm not feeling well all of a sudden, I think I need some air."

She regretted it as soon as she noticed Evelyn's eyes flick from her stomach, to Thane and then back to Grady. Those eyes sparkled even more now.

"I've got to get back to work, Evelyn," Thane said. "We really can't stay."

"Well, I don't want to keep you young things. You'll have your hands full before you know it," she said with a wink. "But just do me a favor and save me a trip out. This needs some witnesses to my signature."

Thane nodded and after she rooted around the TV table next to her, he watched her sign and then took the pen from her and scrawled a quick signature and handed the pen to Grady, his jaw tight, his eyes not meeting hers.

Grady was about to scrawl her own signature just as quickly, but her hand froze as she put the pen to the paper. She was witnessing a living will and 'do not resuscitate order' for Evelyn Hanson. Grady looked up and her eyes caught on a framed photo of Evelyn and ... her husband Jack.

Evelyn patted her hand. "It's okay, honey, we all have to go sometime."

If it had been up to Jack Hanson, Grady would have been gone yesterday, pinned under the blade of his dozer.

"Are you all right?" Evelyn asked, and Grady looked into those concerned eyes.

"Fine," she lied and scribbled her name as close to the line as she could get it with a shaking hand, and dropped the pen.

All she could think of was getting out of that place. She pushed out the door, almost tripped on a loose board in the sagging porch and had to grab the railing to keep from falling, and she stayed like that for a moment. Then she got back into Thane's truck, to be pounced on by Beau. She didn't mind. It was a different kind of being smothered. He smelled like mud and half-digested dog biscuits, and she buried her face in his fur. Anything to get the smell of hospital out of her nose and out of her head. It took a while before she could take a deep breath. It took even longer for Thane to emerge.

She heard the door to the pickup open and close.

"It wasn't my idea," Thane said.

"But you went along with it anyway." She took a ragged breath. "If you're done teaching me a lesson, I'd like to go now."

"If you sue Jack, you wouldn't just be punishing him."

"He deserves to be punished."

"I'm not saying he doesn't. He's an asshole, but his wife isn't. If you ruin him, what would happen to her?"

"I'm not out to ruin anyone," Grady said sullenly.

He didn't comment, except to touch his swollen lip in an unconscious gesture.

Finally he turned the key in the ignition. Grady turned to look out the window.

Thane didn't say a word until they reached his house at the end of the long rutted road. He stopped the truck, but didn't turn it off.

"I've got to meet Cal," he said as he waited for her to unbuckle. "Will you press charges against Jack?" he asked as she got out.

Beau scrambled out after her and she looked down at him as he licked at the back of her hand.

"You really take care of your own around here, don't you?" she said with some bitterness.

"Will you?" he repeated.

"I need to think about it," she said as she closed the door without looking at him.

She turned towards the lake as the truck pulled away slowly.

"I just need to think," she said again to herself. That wasn't coming easily at the moment.

Mike Mullens sat down to the dinner table, late as usual. His wife Susan was so used to it, she didn't usually comment, but tonight she gave him a questioning look.

"Are you fooling around?" she asked suddenly.

"What?!"

He saw her looking at the pale strip of skin on his finger where his ring should have been. In 30 years of marriage he had never removed it, not once. Not even to have it engraved.

He smiled. "I lent it out."

"For a good cause?"

His smile faded. "I hope so. I really hope so." He told her the story of how, against his better judgment, he had united Grady and Thane in holy matrimony.

"Poor Grady," his wife muttered over her tea mug.

The judge laughed out loud. "Poor Grady? She's got a trust fund bigger than the Adirondack Park. I would say, 'Poor Thane!'"

Grady spent the rest of the evening sitting on the bulkhead with Beau watching the lake, the way it changed, the way it took its cue from the sky, always one step behind it, darkening a split second after a cloud covered the sun. She watched ripples form in the sand, and then she'd disturb the temporary sculptures with her toe to watch them form again. The waves kept coming gently, never tiring of their artwork. The water couldn't hold a grudge. Should she?

Whenever she thought of Jack Hanson, all she could see were those oxygen tanks and Evelyn Hanson's bright eyes. The smell of sickness still made her stomach turn. She had no appetite for dinner, which was a good thing, since there wasn't much in Thane's refrigerator or cabinets. When darkness crept up the lengths of the trees and finally turned the sky to ash, Grady went inside.

Beau followed her up to the loft. Grady stripped the bed and left the muddy linens from last night in a neat pile in the corner. Beau laid down on them, yawned and closed his eyes. He wasn't much of a guard dog; he didn't mind at all that she began opening his master's closet and dresser drawers. He had already started to snore. Finally Grady found some clean sheets and pillow- and comforter covers and she made the bed. She changed into flannel pajamas from her overnight bag, went downstairs, and laid down on the couch. She pulled a throw over herself and didn't fall asleep for a long time.

Thane was filthy. He and Cal had been on their hands and knees all afternoon into the evening in crawl spaces turning on water and electric to vacation homes. Nothing had gone as planned. It had been such a tough winter, even where water had been drained, there had been just enough left to pop the joints of pipes during the deepest freeze. If the pipes made it intact, the equipment couldn't handle the change in humidity and temperature. They'd replaced two circulators and one pump today. A house wasn't meant to be empty.

Thane pushed open the door to his cabin, flipped on the light and remembered suddenly his home wasn't empty as Grady Henderson opened her eyes, blinked, and raised herself up on the couch.

"You're back late," she said with a yawn.

"I gave you the bed," Thane said.

"The couch is fine."

"Guests get the bed," he said. "That's how I was raised."

"I'm not a guest," she said looking down. "And besides the way you work, you need your rest."

"Which I'll get on the couch. The bed is yours."

She shrugged and he closed the bathroom door behind him, showered the muck off, put on his sweats and T-shirt that were hanging behind the door and went out to find Grady Henderson asleep again on the couch.

    She was stubborn, but Thane could be too. He picked her up and turned towards the stairs. She didn't wake fully, just enough to put her arms around his back. Her breath was warm against his neck as she mumbled something he couldn't understand. Upstairs he laid her down gently on the bed and pulled the comforter over her. He noticed she had changed the sheets. Beau got up from the pile of dirty laundry in the corner and heaved himself up on the bed to snuggle next to her, and she put her arm around him. He watched the two for a moment more then went downstairs, laid down on the couch that was still warm from Grady's body and tried to fall asleep.

Chapter Four

Thane left the next morning before it got light out and again he came home late, but this time the cabin wasn't dark. He noticed a few things at once as he entered and kicked off his muddy boots. First that Beau didn't come to greet him. The unfaithful dog at Grady's feet turned his head only briefly towards the door, barely thumping his tail. Next Thane noticed the smell of sautéed onions and how hungry he was suddenly. And he noticed his hiking map spread out over the kitchen table.

What he also noticed and what surprised him the most was Grady's expression when she turned from the stove and saw him, as if she were relieved or happy to see him. Then she seemed to remember the situation she was in, that they were in together, and the welcoming smile dropped from her lips.

She saw him glance at the open map. "I didn't mark it up," she said as if already being accused.

He noticed now a stack of newspapers on the floor, the kind that came in his mailbox every week. He usually tossed them into the kindling box next to the woodstove when he was finished with them. Grady had apparently pulled them out, and cut them apart.

Then she had placed pieces of the newspapers on the map. He reached out a hand to turn the map towards him to try to understand a pattern. Maybe Jim was right. Maybe she was crazy.

"No!" Grady called out. She turned the stove off and stepped over to the table. "You'll mess them up."

"What are you doing?" Thane asked. "It looks like a crime scene."

"It is, basically." She leaned over the map. "I got bored, so I started reading through your old newspapers. I even read the police blotters, and you know what I noticed?"

She didn't give him a chance to respond. "There are an awful lot of burglaries around here where nothing valuable gets taken, just things like pots, and food, and blankets, and tools. It doesn't sound like a vandal, it sounds like someone trying to survive out in the woods, and I think I know where his base is. Look, I laid the cut-outs of crime reports over the areas where they happened." She adjusted one of the slips of newsprint and straightened her shoulders. "What do you see?" she asked him.

He shrugged. "A rough circle?"

"Exactly, and what's at the center?"

He shrugged. She pointed at the empty spot between the clippings. The map was topographical, and showed an indent there, but no official roads or trails.

"Hoffman's mine!" she said.

He took a closer look. The garnet mine had been an open pit operation. It had been closed for decades; it wasn't listed on any recent maps.

"How would you know about Hoffman's mine?" Thane asked as he looked up.

"We go back there all the time," she said absently, her eyes still studying the map. "I mean went."

"Evelyn made it sound like you're from here," Thanes said.

"My Dad is from here." She shook her head briefly. "Was from here." Thane noticed the way she kept correcting her tenses. "My Mom came up one summer for vacation from Long Island and they met when their canoes collided. Out there." She tossed her head towards the lake, but her eyes were still attached to the map. "They actually lived up here for a year 'til I was born and 'til my mother couldn't take it any more. Dad had a knack for flipping property and we kept moving south 'til we ended up in Garden City. But we come up every summer. At least Dad and I do." There was that quick shake of the head again. "Did."

They stood there for a few moments, Thane studying Grady's profile, Grady studying the map.

"I know those woods," she said. "And if I were a state trooper, I'd be looking at Hoffman's mine. This is ... was the cabin," She pointed at a spot on the shore of Garnet Lake. "It's a little farther than the rest of these in this circle, but it's still under an hour hike. Or maybe he's moved his home base."

"He?"

"The guy who set fire to the shed by the cabin. The guy who's hiding out in Hoffman's mine." She looked at him thoughtfully. "I mean I'm assuming it's a guy living out there on his own, but I guess it could be a woman. It's got to be somebody. You saw me the whole time. How could I be standing in front of the dozer and setting fire to that shed at the same time?"

"I was wondering the same thing," Thane said.

"You think I did it?"

"I know you didn't."

Grady didn't respond. She didn't take her eyes from the map, but her posture relaxed, as if she no longer had to carry something heavy.

"Are you hungry?" she asked after awhile.

Thane nodded absently, thinking about her theory. She might be right. How to get Opie to see that? He wouldn't accept it, especially coming from her. He watched her in profile as she carefully collected the news clippings in a pile and began folding up the map. She had a delicate nose, high cheekbones and almond-shaped eyes, which narrowed as she glanced up at him.

"I wish you would stop looking at me like that."

"Like what?" he asked.

"Like I'm going to do something crazy."

He touched his lip unintentionally. The swelling had gone down considerably, it no longer tasted like blood.

Her eyes flicked to his lip and she winced. "Maybe I am crazy, or was. I guess I snapped."

When he didn't say anything, she stowed the map and clippings on the counter and turned to the stove and stared down at the headless trout for a moment in the frying pan, before lifting it gingerly onto a plate next to fresh-looking greens and small potatoes.

"I'm not trying to excuse it," she said to the fish as she put the plate on the table in front of Thane and he sat down. From the drawer next to the sink she pulled out silverware and handed it to him. He was surprised at how quickly she had made herself at home here. She sat down next to him at the corner of the table.

"Where did you get all this?" he asked. He had almost nothing in the fridge. He'd meant to go shopping yesterday after work; instead he'd been in court.

She shrugged, still talking to the trout. "We went fishing," she said simply.

"We?"

"Mr. Hardin and I."

"And the salad?" Thane asked as he took a forkful. It was fresh and tart, a tiny bit bitter, but dressed in a perfect mix of vinegar and oil.

"Dandelion greens," she said with a shrug.

He stopped chewing, but only for a moment; he was so hungry, and they were so good.

He looked at her again, trying to reconcile this new information with his first impression. A Long Island princess didn't know about Hoffman's mine, or how to bait a hook, or how to cook weeds. She looked up then, and the way her eyes narrowed, told him she'd misread his gaze.

She sighed. "I'm trying to understand it myself—what happened yesterday. I'm just not in a good place right now. That cabin was the only thing I had left. I know what you're thinking. I've got my trust fund. I mean it's the only thing I have left of my Dad's."

"A thing can be replaced," Thane said. "A person can't."

"That's why it's so hard to let it go! It's like letting him go."

"I wasn't talking about him, I was talking about you. You could have been killed standing up to Jack Hanson and his dozer."

Her shoulders sagged a little. "After Dad died, my mother boxed up all his stuff and gave it to good will. He wasn't even gone a month. She never even asked me if I wanted one of his shirts or even a tie he hated to wear. Do you know how hard it is to hold onto someone when nothing's left? You must think I'm crazy, don't you."

She must think he was stupid to answer a question like that. He took a deep breath.

"I think you're hurting," he said in a voice he tried to make gentle.

He wished he could leave it at that, but he ventured a step further. "And it's natural to want to lash out and hurt someone back," he said slowly. "Like Jack Hanson."

Anger flared in her eyes. "Everyone's so worried about him! Who's going to keep me from getting hurt?"

He fixed her with a hard look. "I did my best."

She dropped her head for just a moment, and when she looked up again the anger was gone. She reminded him so much of the lake, the way it changed from one moment to the next. "I never thanked you for that—for saving my life," she said.

"You still haven't." He attempted a smile, but it turned into a grimace around his split lip, and she looked at him uncertainly. "Forget about it," he said.

She put a hand suddenly on his arm. "No, I'm grateful. I am. I don't know how I can repay something like that."

"Don't press charges against Jack Hanson."

She looked down. "Okay," she said to the table top.

"Okay?" he repeated as if he hadn't heard her right.

"I mean it, I won't press charges. Whatever you think of me, I mean what I say."

Her hand still lay on his forearm. He felt the warmth of it. Her eyes seemed to catch on the wedding band he wore before rising to meet his stare. Her words had come out with conviction. Her expression seemed conflicted. She'd already made one promise that she planned to break with a divorce. Could he trust her in anything else?

The next night Thane came home to a dark and empty cabin. He wouldn't admit to himself that he'd gotten used to having company. He tried to think instead what the judge would do to him if Grady had made a run for it on Thane's watch—and on Beau's. Wherever Grady had gone, Beau had obviously gone with her, the old traitor.

Thane didn't immediately go searching for them, because he'd noticed a pot simmering on the stove and walked over to turn it off. He lifted the lid to find what must have been venison stew. It was the only meat he'd had left in the freezer. He helped himself to a bowl. Venison could be tough and gamey if you didn't know how to prepare it. A second helping convinced him that Grady Henderson of all people knew how to cook it. He put the bowl in the sink and left the cabin.

A long way off, in the direction of Dan Hardin's house, he heard a familiar bark.

The day had been warm again, but the evening was recovering the spring chill, and Thane enjoyed the crisp air as he walked the rutted road to his neighbor's house.

He found Dan out back stripping long sheets of birch bark from a tree propped up on wooden horses. Thane had dragged it here to give the old man something to do. Grady sat not far from him on a stump beside a small fire with Beau resting at and on her feet. Her head was bowed as she fidgeted with a jagged piece of birch bark. Next to her was a rough messy stack of scraps.

Thane stood for a moment, outside the light of the fire, listening to the melodies of Dan's gruff voice and the contrast of her light laughter. Dan only liked a handful of people, and in Thane's experience never openly showed his affection. Here he was different. A smile made his face younger. Or had the old bastard shaved the perennial stubble from his chin? Of all the people to make a change in him—Grady? They were both stubborn. As he watched her, she tossed the birch bark into the fire, and the image of a cabin lit up as the piece started to burn. In a long stride Thane was at the fire, pulling the piece of bark out of the flames by one unsinged corner.

"Ya darn fool!" Dan's voice was harsh. "That's hotter than hell's handles. Anyone teach you to not play with fire?"

"This from a man who cleans the inside of his chimney by setting it ablaze."

"I'd like to set fire to your rear end with a strip of hickoy."

Thane ignored the old man's tirade as he pulled another piece of bark from the fire.

He turned to Grady. "I can't believe you would just throw this away."

Running a finger over the etching of a rustic cabin, he couldn't tell where her artificial rendering of smoke from its chimney ended, and where the natural rough edge of wood began.

Her shoulders were rigid in their defensiveness. "Mr. Hardin said it was too small for you to use. I won't do it again."

Thane shook his head. "You don't understand. I want you to do it again. Come with me, I need to show you something."

When she didn't follow, he grabbed her hand and pulled her up from the stump.

Dan Hardin began to mutter something about young folk these days and manners, but Thane didn't stop to listen to the whole sermon.

"Where are you going?" Grady asked Thane as she stumbled along after him in the growing darkness.

"You'll see in a minute." He'd been going nowhere with his rustic furniture. She had just given him an idea that could take him somewhere.

Grady could barely keep up with Thane as he pulled her along beside him. The dirt road from Dan's house was uneven, and she stumbled a few times, but his hand kept her from falling. He didn't release her, even as he finally stopped in front of his old barn on the crest of the hill above his cabin. With one hand he flipped the latch open and gave the door a violent push, sending it screeching back. Beau hung back until Thane reached into the darkness and pulled on a long wire and a bulb sent out an insufficient light, like a weak sun in a vast solar system. It illuminated an assortment of rustic furniture made of cedar, pine and birch. The crowning piece was a bed, the frame painstakingly lined with twigs alternating between the bony white and deep burgundy of paper and river birch. Two thick posts of birch on either side retained their branches intertwining above like a canopy. It was intricate and simple at the same time and she imagined the work that must have gone into it to make it seem natural and above all alive.

"You made these?"

He nodded. "I didn't realize what was missing, until tonight."

His grip became even tighter and she looked down at her hand entwined in his. She felt suddenly anchored and after being adrift for so long, coming to a stop was disorienting. She was so aware of his calloused hand, so aware of him, yet she found it hard to concentrate on what he was saying. He was missing something. She knew what that was like.

"But these are perfect," she said quietly. "What could be missing?"

"You."

She looked up. His brown eyes were earnest, all his attention focused on her. Her heart seemed to go into freefall and she thought it would never stop falling. But then he finished his sentence and it came crashing to a stop. "Your artwork. I want you to etch a scene on the birch along the headboard. Could you do that?"

"I ... I'd be afraid to touch it. And what kind of scene?"

He shrugged. "Whatever you want, as long as you can finish it in two weeks. I entered it in the Rustic Furniture Fair competition at the Adirondack Museum over in Blue Mountain Lake. Please Grady, say yes. This is the edge I need. Will you do this?"

He had never said this much to her at once. She was overwhelmed by it, by the emotion in his voice, by the feeling of his hand on hers.

"Will you?" he repeated. "Please."

Yes. She owed him, didn't she? She'd gotten him involved in her own troubles and the least she could do was help him while she was here. Of course she'd do it. That answer rose up inside her, but she didn't let it out because she knew as soon as she said it, he would let her go. She didn't want him to let her go, ever. She looked at the wide pale swatch of birch, so pristine she couldn't bear to touch it. What could it look like? Her mind filled with various scenes. What could Grady's life look like? Before she could stop her imagination it put pictures in her head that she couldn't get out, didn't want to get out. And they all had to do with the man standing beside her, holding her hand.

Thane was waiting for an answer. Finally, she nodded.

And then he let her go.

Chapter Five

Grady had only been in Thane's house three days, but already she had a morning ritual. She'd take a cup of coffee from the pot he had made before he left. Then she'd go out to the dock, stick her feet in the water, and watch the mist uncover the lake. Today, she didn't linger by the lake; there was work to do, which might explain why Thane had taken Beau with him, so he wouldn't distract her.

She made her way up the steep hill to the barn and shoved the door aside. Unlike Thane, she had to put her coffee cup down and use both hands and lean on it with all her strength. The sun was shy and stayed behind as she entered, but its light filtered through the slits in the barn board dappling the saw dust on the dirt floor.

She wandered for awhile around the barn, peering into old feed boxes, some of them still stuffed with hay. In an old stall in the corner she found some rough wooden carvings strewn on a rickety table. Underneath the table was a water-stained box. She reached for it wondering if there were more little sculptures inside, but stopped herself. Thane had told her in no uncertain terms he didn't want her in his business. She studied the figures on the table instead. Thane must have whittled them from leftover blocks of wood, a fawn in a reclining position, a fat-bellied bird, and a dog. Grady recognized Beau immediately in the last one and she picked up his likeness and turned it over and over in her hands as she wandered back to the main bay in the barn.

She sat for a moment on a low-slung bench, and her hand came to rest on the birch backrest. She rubbed a thumb over it, following the flow of its unfinished lines. Thane had left his red toolbox on the floor of the barn and she put the carving of Beau down and rummaged through it not really knowing what she was looking for until she found an awl. Soon it's sharp point was not so much etching something new on the blank space of the bench as uncovering what was there already.

She didn't know what time it was when she finally stopped and stretched. She had a crick in her neck, and she couldn't tell if she was still sore from wrestling with a state trooper and being cuffed, or from bending over her work today. She walked back to the cabin and rummaged in the near-empty fridge for some lunch. When the phone rang, she picked it up without thinking.

A voice she recognized was demanding Thane.

"He's not here, Cal, I thought he was working for you," Grady said.

"He is," he said. "But he's out of cell range, so I need you tell him to meet me at the Blackburns as soon as he gets in."

"As soon as he gets in, he'll be eating dinner."

There was a pause. "Well maybe between the main course and dessert, you could give him my message ... Mrs. McMasters."

Without another word, she slammed the phone down. Mrs. McMasters! She wasn't anyone's wife except in name. She didn't belong to anyone. And she wasn't sure how she felt about that.

Thane came home early for the first time in months. Grady hadn't looked up when he pulled to a stop in front of the open barn door. He got out of the truck and stood for a moment looking at the bedframe he had crafted. The headboard was as blank and empty as last night. He would have been disappointed, but his eyes caught on the bench next to it.

A river ran its course through cattails and rushes along the backrest of the bench, entwined in the irregularities of the bark.

He stood there for a long time until Beau stuck his snout between Grady and her artwork and she jumped.

She laughed and rubbed the dog vigorously behind the ear. It took her awhile to notice Thane and she looked up, her open happy expression turning more guarded.

"What do you think?" she said as she stood up.

"It's beautiful."

She smiled down at the tool in her hand.

"It's quitting time," Thane said as he took the awl from her.

"You've done enough work today."

"Oh," she said suddenly. "Speaking of work."

"What?"

She looked hard at him for a moment, before glancing away. "You look tired," she said. "You're working too hard."

She was right. He was beat. Two nights of sleeping on an uncomfortable couch hadn't helped. But right now he didn't feel tired as he looked at the work Grady had done. He helped her stow the tools back in the box.

He picked up the carving he'd done of Beau, whittled on a long winter's night. "Where'd you find this?" he asked.

She nodded towards the old stall. "You should sell them," she said.

"It's just scrap," he said, and he pulled his arm back, to see if he could chuck it over the low wall and back onto the table, but she grabbed it from his hand.

"Don't, he's keeping me company."

"I should have left the real Beau with you if you're afraid to be out here by yourself."

"Why would I be afraid?" she asked as she leaned down to latch the toolbox.

He looked at her. She wasn't afraid of anything. It had gotten her into trouble with a state trooper. He didn't want her getting into any more trouble. With the recent burglaries, it wouldn't be a bad idea to leave Beau with her. It would be safer. A question popped into his head. Safer for her, or for a burglar who wouldn't realize what he was up against in Grady Henderson?

Grady set the rough sculpture of Beau on top of the toolbox and turned to him "What's so funny?" she asked.

He erased the half-smile that had hijacked his mouth. "Nothing," he said.

As he was sliding the big door closed, he heard the beeping of a horn and turned to see Cal's pickup coming around the bend and screeching to a halt in front of him and Grady.

Cal got out and looked over his hood at Thane. "You didn't get my message?"

They both looked at Grady, who was looking down at the gravelly road beneath her feet. She kicked at a small stone and sent it flying.

"What message?" Thane asked. "Grady?"

She shrugged.

Cal answered for her. "The message she didn't bother to give you that I need you over at the Blackburns. Now!"

"You want him there, you don't need him there," Grady said. "You're taking advantage of him."

Cal rocked back on his heels. "Me? What about you. You married him for money, for God's sake."

"For the record I married him for my money! Not his," Grady said. "And believe me, it will be worth his while."

Cal looked her up and down. "I'm sure it will be," he said with a wide smile.

Thane saw the storm grow in her eyes.

"Grady, would you do me a favor and make me a cup of coffee to take along?"

Instinctively he reached out and touched her gently on the shoulder. It was rigid.

"Please?" he added lowly. Her shoulder relaxed under his hand. Was it that easy? He realized she wasn't used to being asked nicely.

"I'll take a cup too, darlin'," Cal called after her as she passed him.

Grady froze for just a moment before moving stiffly towards the cabin door.

"I like it sweet like my women," Cal continued, chuckling.

"Knock it off, Cal," Thane said loudly enough for Grady to hear, and was relieved when he saw her disappear through the cabin door. With a bang.

"What? I'm just having fun."

"At the expense of everything you've worked for."

"What's she going to do? Marry me?"

"She'll put a lien on the construction. She's impulsive and she's angry, and she thinks she has nothing to lose."

"I'm not worried, you seem to be able to handle her," he said, emphasizing the word 'handle.' "And besides, she doesn't have to stop construction, because I've already stopped it."

"Why the hell?"

"I thought she would have told you. Because she asked me to, nicely. $50,000 is pretty nice, isn't it?"

"Where'd she get that kind of money?"

"Don't know, don't care."

"She could have used it as bail money," Thane said out loud.

Cal's perpetual grin got wider. "Maybe she likes playing house with you. She seems pretty comfy here."

Thane swallowed a response. "What about the money you're going to lose by not building Hartwell his mansion?"

"Who knows if they ever would have gotten approval from the Adirondack Park Agency anyway."

"You told me they had approval!"

"I said they as good as had approval. Hartwell sits on some board with some ex-politician somewhere."

"Damn it, Cal! I agreed to marry Grady Henderson to protect your project that you didn't even really have. I threw myself on a grenade for you!"

"For us," Cal corrected him. "We're as good as partners, remember? And at least it's a good-looking grenade. More like an H-bomb from what Opie said. Bet she's a little firecracker in—"

"Shut up!" Thane said. "Don't say another word about her."

Cal's eyes narrowed as his grin widened. "Maybe she's not the only one who enjoys playing house."

"I'm warning you."

Cal shrugged. "Speaking of houses, we're going to build the Blackburns a huge one with a detached garage, and a boat house."

"We're going to really build it, or as good as build it?" Thane asked.

"That's where you come in. We're meeting with them now, and they're going to tell you exactly what they want, and you're going to come up with the drawings, except bigger and better."

"I don't work that way, Cal, you know that."

He sighed. "I know, but your drawings will impress the hell out of them anyway, and then I'll start bringing in the money."

"And what will I get?" Thane asked.

"Rid of Grady Henderson for one," he said. "So you better enjoy it while it lasts."

Grady came up the sharp incline from the cabin then and handed each of them a Styrofoam cup.

"Is there sugar in it?" Cal was asking.

"Sure is, darlin'," Grady said frostily.

Cal took a sip and spit it out and his face turned sour for a moment.

"Too sweet?" Grady asked.

"Nothing can be too sweet," Cal responded, but with not as much humor as before.

Thane took a cautious sip from his own cup. It was exactly the way he liked it.

When Thane woke the next morning it was already light out. He swung his feet off the couch, sat up and rubbed his hands over his face. He needed a shave. He needed a damned vacation.

He only noticed now that Grady sat in the chair opposite the couch, one hand absently rubbing Beau's ear, while they both watched him. She looked away as soon as he looked up, and she seemed very interested in the cold woodstove in the corner.

"What time is it?" Thane asked groggily.

"9:00ish," she said to the stove.

"Why didn't this go off?!" he asked as he reached over to the side table, and checked the small alarm. He was sure he'd turned it on last night. "Grady? Did you turn this off?"

She looked down at Beau. "You got in really late last night."

"You can't just turn my alarm off!" Thane got up and took the circular steps to the loft two at a time. He had worked on the Blackburn plans until midnight, but still had to print them out this morning before he and Cal would meet the couple. He pulled jeans from a drawer until he found a pair without holes or paint stains, and he grabbed a collared shirt from the closet and put them on.

"You can't keep working like this," Grady called from below.

She was right; he'd have to work even harder.

"Cal told me you paid him $50,000 to stop construction," he called down. "Where'd you get that kind of money? I thought you said you couldn't touch your trust for a month."

"I borrowed it from my lawyer," she said as he came down. She was staring out the window onto the lake,

"You could have made bail." he said.

She shrugged.

"You could have been gone already," he said.

She turned to him as he sat down on the bench by the door and started putting on his boots.

"Do you want me gone?" she asked.

"No," he said. "I don't."

She looked away from him to the table, where he noticed now a plate of scrambled eggs and an English muffin. "Aren't you going to eat breakfast?" she asked.

"I don't have time."

"You need to make time."

She sandwiched the eggs between the bread and handed it to him. Then she began putting on her sneakers.

"Where are you going?" Thane asked.

"I thought you could drop me in town," she said. "I need some stuff."

At least it was on his way. Cal was working out of a trailer a mile past town.

They drove in silence. When he pulled in front of the grocery store, she didn't get out right away.

"Grady, I'm in a hurry."

"Um. Do you think I could borrow something from you?"

"What?" he asked.

"Um. Some money."

"Don't you have credit cards?"

"Yeah, but I'd rather use cash."

"Why?"

She didn't answer right away, and Thane didn't have time to get into it. He sighed and reached into his back pocket for his wallet, took out a couple bills and handed them to her.

"I'll pay you back," she said sheepishly.

"Don't worry about it. You can work it off. I owe you more than that for the work you've done already."

"No, you don't."

"Grady, I don't have time to argue. I'll try to swing by in an hour and pick you up. Hopefully I'll have time to drop you back home."

He grabbed Beau by the collar as he tried to follow Grady out of the truck, and the dog whined about it the whole way to Cal's office. It was going to be a long day.

Grady stood for a moment watching Thane drive off and then looked down at the bills in her hand and folded them and put them into the pocket of her jeans. Her mother would find out where she was eventually, but right now Grady didn't want to be found. Not using her credit cards was a silly precaution. Her mother would never bother trying to find her, especially not while on her honeymoon with Richard Hartwell.

As the doors to the small supermarket opened automatically in front of her and her cart vibrated over the threshold she thought ironically that this was her own honeymoon.

Grady put the few things she needed in the cart and thought about Thane's empty refrigerator. Conscious of how much she had to spend, she went up and down the narrow aisles studying the items on the shelves. She was shopping for her husband and had no idea what he liked to eat.

At the checkout, she didn't pay attention to the family in front of her as the mother with two kids unloaded an overflowing shopping cart onto the conveyor belt. Grady was looking at her own cart, adding up the items in her head to make sure she didn't go over budget. She didn't look up until a bag of frozen spinach came sailing into the cart and landed on the chicken she was going to buy.

"Shhhh!" the little boy in front of her was saying. "I hate spinach."

"Jordan!" He might have hoped it would stay his and Grady's secret, but his mother was already fishing it from Grady's cart and dropping it on the counter.

"I'm sorry," she said as she glanced up from the chaos in front of her. And then she looked back again with wide, uncertain eyes.

"Grady Henderson?"

"Shauna Evans??"

It was not easy to squeeze past the carts to hug each other, but they managed. Grady didn't want to let her go, but they pulled away and held each other at arm's length as if trying to reconcile a 10-year-old mental snapshot with the present.

"It's not Evans any more," Shauna said laughing. "It's ... cut that out!" She interrupted herself, grabbing a bag of candy her son had pulled off the rack and had been about to rip open. She stuffed it back onto the shelf.

"What are you doing here?" Grady and Shauna said at the same time.

"It's a long story," Grady said.

"Mine too. How long will you be here?" Shauna asked.

Grady didn't know how to answer that. "A month." Until she made bail! "How about you?"

"For forever," Shauna said with a laugh. "I married into the Adirondacks." Without commenting, without even looking, she grabbed a bag of gummi bears from another small set of hands and put them back on the rack.

"Your boys are beautiful!" Grady said.

"Thanks," Shauna said "They look just like their Dad." But then she winced. "Except he's not looking so pretty right now. He had an accident at work. Speaking of which, he's getting off shift soon and he's going to be famished."

"Does he work at the paper mill?"

"No, he's ... that is not a quarter, you're going to jam it!" she shouted at the younger of her boys who had found his way to the gumball machine.

Grady helped her old friend load her groceries into her cart.

"You're staying at the lake?" Shauna assumed.

Yes, but not where she should have been.

"That is your last warning, mister!" Shauna called to her son who had begun shaking the gumball machine to get the coin out. Then she turned back to Grady. "I can get my in-laws to watch the boys tonight. Let's meet at The Well and catch up! How's 7:00?"

Shauna didn't wait for an answer. She gave Grady another tight hug and then she was gone in a whirlwind of sticky hands and bags and commotion.

Grady watched her go with a big smile. She'd thought she'd lost everything from her past. She'd been wrong.

When Thane pulled in front of the grocery store he was relieved to see Grady waiting for him outside. He got out and helped her load the bags into the bed of the pickup. He didn't bother asking her for change from the bills he'd given her.

As he stopped at the one traffic light in town where the main street intersected route 9, he glanced at her. She looked different. She was smiling. Her eyes were bright.

"You'll never guess what happened," she said. "I ran into an old friend."

It surprised him almost that she'd have friends.

"I haven't seen her in ten years. Her uncle used to rent a cottage at Gull's every summer, just around the point from my Dad's cabin. We used to catch frogs together when we were kids! But then the rentals got sold and torn down and we lost track of each other. She was from Queens, but she ended up marrying a guy up here, can you believe it?"

The light changed, and Thane's thoughts turned back to the Blackburn plans and what kind of questions they might ask him. He nodded mechanically as Grady reminisced.

"It's such a small world, isn't it?" she said when they reached his house and she got out.

"Hmm," Thane murmured.

If he had paid attention, he would have realized it was a very small world. Downright claustrophobic.

When Thane came back to the cabin in the evening, Grady was standing at the door and opened it for him.

"Oh, there you are. I didn't want to be late for dinner."

"Dinner?" He had assumed she'd be cooking, considering all the food she'd bought that morning—with his money.

"At The Well. To meet my friend. Remember, I told you I ran into her in the store this morning? I asked you if you could take me and you said yes."

"I did?"

"You nodded."

Thane didn't remember agreeing to anything, but then again he hadn't been paying attention. The last thing he wanted to do was go out. But he had to eat, didn't he? And he could sure use a beer. He sighed and pushed the door open for Grady. She had put her hair back from her eyes with a clip, and they were bright as she passed him. But her smile was the accessory that seemed to soften her. She tilted her head and gave him a questioning look as they stood on either side of the threshold.

"What are you waiting for?" she asked.

"Nothing," he said, as he closed the door behind him without locking it.

She blocked his way for a moment. "Aren't you afraid someone will get in?" she asked.

Someone already had. He looked down into her eyes made brighter by the porch light. No lock on earth was going to do him a damned bit of good.

Chapter Six

The Well had a sagging wrap-around porch full of tables that didn't match, littered with beer bottles that hadn't yet been cleaned up. Nothing had changed since Grady's Dad would bring her here after a day of fishing on the Schroon River. The smoky haze that seemed to float above the two billiard tables in the back was gone, but that didn't lift the darkness that made Grady think of a bear's den. She searched for Shauna with an expectant smile which died as she spied Judge Mullens standing at the corner of the bar.

Thane leaned across the bar to place an order and she approached the judge.

"Your old fishing buddy sends his regards," Grady said.

He accepted two long-necked bottles of Genesee Beer from the bartender, clenched them together in one fist, and took a step towards towards her. She didn't move aside.

"Sorry, Mrs. McMasters, you'll have to be more specific."

"Fred Morey."

The judge chuckled. "So, he's your attorney. Must be why you haven't sued me yet."

"You can't fish with all the lawyers in New York."

"That's right. I hunt too." He looked down at her. "Are you going to get out of my way?"

"Are you going to get out of mine?"

He laughed. "I heard you could have been out of here already. That you had the money for bail and you gave it to Cal Sterling. Giving money to Cal is not my idea of a sound investment."

"Tell that to Thane."

"I did, but back then he thought friendship was more important than money. I wonder if that's still true."

Grady's eyes narrowed. "You could have let me go instead of remanding me to his care. You got him into this."

"Maybe you'll be the one to get him out of it."

"How?"

"I don't know, Mrs. McMasters. I don't have the answers. Hell, I don't even have the right questions. Now if you don't mind, I'd like to drink these with my wife in peace."

Grady took a step out of his way, and it changed her perspective. She spotted Shauna sitting at the table behind the judge, and she smiled again. She couldn't see her husband's face, because it was buried in Shauna's rich, wavy hair as he nuzzled her neck. But Grady recognized that build, the thick arm slung around her friend's shoulder. Her smile died in an instant. From the corner of her eye, Grady saw the judge turn to follow her gaze.

He raised the bottles as if in a toast and walked away. "Enjoy your evening," he said in passing. "I'm sure I will."

Thane paid for the two bottles of Genny Cream Ale and turned from the bar. Grady stood like a statue with her back to him, but she turned suddenly towards him.

"This wasn't a good idea," she said quickly. "Let's go."

"But I just got these drinks."

He heard Grady's name being called, and looked over her head to see Shauna Oplin standing up and taking the few steps towards them. At the same time, her husband Jim froze with a bottle of beer halfway to his open mouth. He slammed the bottle down and a volcano of foam spurted out the top.

Thane was too surprised to curse, or turn around and leave. He'd regret that. Shauna was already pulling Grady to the table and pushing her down and taking a seat across from her. Thane followed them and sat down rigidly across from Jim, and put the beer bottles on the table.

"Grady, this is my husband, Jim," Shauna said happily. Then her smile dimmed as she noticed the way Jim and Grady stared at each other across the table.

"Do you two know each other?" she said slowly.

Neither of them spoke, but they both looked down at the table now.

"You've met?" Shauna pressed.

"The other day," Grady said quietly.

Shauna turned to her husband. "Where?"

He cleared his throat. "At work."

Shauna looked back and forth between the two for a moment and then her eyes widened.

"Grady is not the Long Island princess who broke your nose!" she said in disbelief. "Is she?"

Jim cursed. "Who told you that, because I sure didn't."

"Jack Hanson was there. Your aunt bowls with Evelyn Hanson's nurse," Shauna said, her eyes still wide and focused on Grady. "But it couldn't be Grady they were talking about. You wouldn't do something like that, Grady. Would you?"

Grady was still studying the scratched table top. "It was an accident," she said.

"Accident?" Jim said in a loud voice. Heads turned at the other tables. Thane was glad when the jukebox began to thump with an old country song.

The waitress came and began handing out menus. Grady refused one.

"I lost my appetite," she said without looking up.

Shauna put a restraining hand on her husband's arm, and at the same time leaned in to Grady and somehow got her to look at the menu. Shauna ordered a plate of chicken wings and told the waitress they needed more time.

What they needed was to get out of there.

Jim leaned towards Thane. "What the hell were you thinking bringing her here?"

"Me?! Shauna didn't tell you you were meeting up with Grady Henderson?"

Jim shrugged. "She was going on and on about some old friend. I guess I just tuned it out."

Thane didn't say anything. He'd done the same thing with Grady, too preoccupied with the Blackburn bid to pay attention to what she was saying—to what they were getting into.

"Why didn't I see your car in the parking lot?" Thane asked.

"So, what, you're avoiding me now?"

"Wouldn't you have wanted that?"

"We left our car at my folks, because it has the car seats in it—they're watching the kids—and we took theirs," he said. "You're not hungry," he added in a low tone. "Drink up and get her the hell out of here, or I will." Jim put his bottle of Genesee to his lips and Thane watched the bottle empty much too quickly.

When the waitress came back and set the appetizer down in front of them, Thane asked her to take it back and wrap it up 'to go.'

"I still have some work to do," he said as soon as she was gone, but he didn't need to make an excuse. No one protested. Shauna was the only one talking. She'd been taking a beautician course in Glens Falls and her final exam was the next morning. Jim's aunt had volunteered reluctantly to be her guinea pig and Shauna would have to cut her hair in front of a panel of judges. Shauna was saying she wasn't sure who was more nervous, herself, or Jim's aunt.

Grady nodded, but Thane was sure she hadn't heard a word.

"How did you two ever meet?" Grady said, suddenly turning to Shauna.

Jim answered for her. "I caught her speeding. I told her I'd drop all the charges if she slept with me."

Shauna smacked his arm. "That's not how it went. Not exactly, anyway."

Jim shrugged. "Jordan was born nine months later, wasn't he?"

"So you had to marry him," Grady said.

Jim leaned forward. "Shauna didn't have to do anything. She wanted to."

Grady shook her head ever so slightly and snorted derisively.

"Know what I want to do right now?" he said.

"I'm guessing not your job, or you'd be hiking into Hoffman's mine to find that guy who's been setting fires."

Jim cocked his head. "What the hell do you know about Hoffman's mine?"

"More than you do apparently. Most of the vandalism around here happens within an hour's radius from Hoffman's mine. Try reading the police blotters in the newspapers, you could learn a lot. Or have someone read them to you."

Jim stood up so suddenly his chair toppled over. Within a second, Thane and Shauna were standing too, each of them with a hand on his arm on either side of him. Grady sat looking up at him, picking up her beer and drinking it without breaking eye contact.

"We're going," Thane said to Grady.

"But the waitress hasn't come back with our food," she said.

Thane let go of Jim and put a hand on Grady's arm and pulled her up.

"You said you weren't hungry," he reminded her gruffly.

He ignored Judge Mullens's quizzical look as they passed. He noticed the judge hold Jim back, and he was grateful for the head start.

Once outside, Thane took a deep breath, and let Grady go. He should have known from past experience that was a mistake. Shauna came out and blocked their way, her hands on her hips.

"Grady, what's gotten into you?" she said.

"Shauna, I'm sorry. I just haven't been dealing with everything so well," she stammered. "My Dad. He's gone. And my Mom—she just got married again."

Shauna's tone changed. "Oh, Grady, I'm sorry! I didn't know they finally split up."

"No!" Grady said. "It's not like that. He didn't leave us ... I mean, I guess he did in a way. He's gone," she said again. "Forever." The last word came out in a whisper.

"You mean passed away? Oh Grady, I'm so sorry. I didn't know. He was so young. What happened?"

"She gave him a stroke," Jim muttered as he pushed the screen door open and stalked out onto the porch.

Grady turned in an instant and before Thane could react, she threw herself towards Jim and grabbed his shirt with both hands.

"Take it back, you bastard."

"Did she just lay a hand on me?" Jim asked with false surprise.

"Did she just call me what I think she called me?" He turned back and forth to Thane and Shauna causing Grady to stumble, but she didn't let go.

He looked down at her, and an ugly smirk spread across his bruised face. "Dreams really do come true," he said. And then his voice dropped. "I would advise you to remove your hands from my person."

"I would advise you to take back what you said," Grady spat back.

"I'm warning you," Jim said, but even before he finished speaking, he broke her hold on his shirt, bent her arm behind her back and slammed her against the rough wooden siding of the building. Her hip hit one of the un-bussed tables and a beer bottle tipped off the edge and crashed to the porch floor.

"Jim, let her go," Shauna said.

"As soon as she apologizes for breaking my nose."

"I'm sorry," Grady panted through a grimace. "That you don't know how to do your job."

Jim increased the pressure on her arm, and she grunted. With her right hand, her only free hand, Grady struck out blindly to the table next to her, knocking another empty bottle to the floor. Her hand found an overturned bottle and she grabbed it by its neck.

"Oh, this just keeps getting better and better," Jim said. "Go ahead. Do it. I'm begging you."

But he didn't give her a chance. He squeezed her wrist until she dropped the bottle, then he brought her hands together, reached behind him to his belt and pulled off a pair of handcuffs and clicked them in place.

Thane grabbed him by the shoulder. "That's enough, Jim! Let her go."

Now his friend's surprise was genuine. "You've got to be freaking kidding me."

Grady started to push herself away from the wall, but Jim put his right hand just below her neck and pushed her back. He was still staring at Thane.

"You've been with her, what, four days and she's already got your head turned around. And I'm not talking about this head." With his free hand, Jim tapped his own temple.

Shauna was pulling at his elbow on his other side. "Jim, this does not look good, please!"

"It looks great to me," he said.

Shauna was reaching into her husband's pocket and pulling out his set of keys.

He stared at her with wide eyes as if she'd betrayed him, but he didn't stop her as she moved around him and uncuffed Grady.

Grady turned from the wall, rubbing her wrists. Her face was red, but one cheek was brighter than the other where it had scraped against the rough siding.

She did not appear grateful for Thane and Shauna stepping in.

She took a step closer to Jim. "You are going to regret this," she seethed.

Thane watched his friend's chest expand, but he didn't wait for him to respond. The porch creaked as Thane lifted Grady by the waist and carried her down the steps. He heard Jim's heavy tread follow them on the sagging stairs, but he didn't stop until he reached the truck and put Grady down not so gently against the passenger's side door. He leaned in, one hand on the hood, the other against the door frame, enclosing her. Inside the cab, Beau woke up suddenly and threw himself at the window in excitement.

"You're standing on the Horicon line," Jim said behind them. "I can haul your ass up to Judge Tremont. He won't go so easy on you with some half-assed homestay that seems to have turned into a goddamned honeymoon."

"You know all about half-assed," Grady said as she tried to push past Thane.

"Get in the truck," Thane said to her. Behind him he heard Shauna urging her husband to get into their car.

"I'm not finished," Grady said.

"Yes you are, damn it!" Thane told her. Something in his voice surprised her, took her attention away from Jim and she turned her narrowed eyes on him. "You're going to get in the truck, and then we're going to go home," Thane said

"You can't tell me what to do!" Grady said.

Thane looked down at her. He was past telling her. In a minute he was going to pick her up again and throw her into the truck.

Jim's angry voice could be heard across the parking lot. "You think she's a friend, Shauna? She'll use you, like she's using Thane," he went on. Then his voice got even louder. "I hope you're at least getting some, buddy. I hope it's worth it."

Grady heaved herself away from the truck at that, but Thane's body acted as a barrier. He held her there pinned against the door even after he heard Opie's tires spin in the parking lot spraying the back of his shins with gravel like shrapnel.

"Get in the truck," he said gruffly. She didn't move. He squeezed his eyes shut for a moment and summoned every ounce of self control he had left. "Please," he said through gritted teeth.

Grady's shoulders sagged. Thane moved away to open the passenger side door, and then the voice behind him made Grady go all rigid again.

"Well, if it isn't the honeymooners," Judge Mullens chuckled as he passed them, arm in arm with his wife. "Glad to see married life is having a stabilizing influence on you, Mrs. McMasters."

Thane pushed Grady into the cab before she could say anything, shut the door and leaned against it with all his weight. "You got me into this. Do you have to make it harder than it already is?" Thane said tightly.

Judge Mullens gave a short laugh. "I'm not the one who proposed."

"Neither was I," Thane said under his breath, as he pulled the keys from his pocket.

Mike Mullens got into the passenger's side of his Honda Civic and handed the keys to his wife in the driver's side, despite the fact he was suddenly sober.

"I hope you know what you're doing," she said as she started the car.

"I don't have the slightest idea."

They rode home in silence, the headlights barely touching the outlines of evergreens that pressed in along the sides of the road. At home he kissed his wife goodnight and went to his den and sat under the reproachful glassy eyes of the ten-point buck he'd snagged 30 years ago, on a hunting trip with Will Henderson—Grady's father.

From the bottom drawer of his desk he pulled out a letter. He felt his shirt pocket for his reading glasses, before he remembered he'd left them at the office. He didn't really need them; he knew the incomplete sentences of the letter by heart.

Mike,

I saw the doctor, like you've been bugging me to do. It's not good news. They could give me a year with operations and filling me up with poison, but it would be a year of dying, and I'd rather take three months of living. I'm not worried about me, or Sandra, she'll be all right. But Grady...

All these years I taught her everything I knew about surviving. If I dropped her out in the woods, I know she'd be able to make a fire, find food. I did my best to teach her to protect herself from anything that would hurt her. I never thought I'd be the one, in the end, to cause her this much pain.

And I don't know how I'm going to tell her all this. She's not afraid of anything. The problem is, I am! Of losing her.

I've tried to put it in a letter for her, but how can you put that much love into words? Maybe when we get up to the cabin, it will be easier to tell her. I don't know.

You know she's got a habit of running away. I hope, if she does after I'm gone that she'll run to the right place. She loves that cabin on Garnet Lake as much as I do. I hope she finds some peace there. It's easier to find there than anywhere. She's provided for. At least as far as money goes. But she needs more than money.

We take care of our own in Garnet Lake, we always have. If Grady runs ... when she runs, would you be there for me? Would you be there to catch her, if I can't?

Mike Mullens was a good judge. He was a better hunter. But none of those skills would help him to get Grady Henderson to stay put.

He glanced up at the mounted buck on his wall. "Don't look at me like that," he muttered before rubbing his eyes and putting his head in his hands.

There was no trap Grady Henderson couldn't get out of, even if it meant hurting herself to do it, like a fox that gnaws its own leg to escape. Would a wedding band be strong enough to hold her? He rubbed the spot on his finger where the gold ring he'd loaned to Thane was missing. It made him think of his own wilder days when he had imagined nothing could settle him. That simple gold band had been enough to ground him. Would it work for Grady?

Thane turned the radio on in the truck, but no sound came out. He listened instead to Beau's insecure whining. Grady, thankfully, didn't say a word the whole way home from The Well.

The altercation outside the bar wasn't the first. It had been a rougher place when he and Jim and Cal were growing up. They'd gotten into their share of scrapes. The difference was tonight, Thane hadn't sided with his best friend.

Thane had grown up assuming nothing could come between them. But tonight after all these years something had. Someone had. Grady Henderson. Jim was right. She was turning Thane's head around. He glanced at her. Beau was at her feet looking up at her, but her eyes were on her hands. She was turning that garnet ring—the wedding ring—around and around on her finger.

Thane turned his eyes back to the road. He couldn't trust her to keep her feelings in check. He was angry at himself for the same reason.

Thane parked in front of the barn, got out of the truck, slammed the door and headed down the steep path to his house without waiting for Grady. It was a dark night. She looked up at the sky, but even the stars didn't want to be around. Beau ran ahead, and she felt suddenly deserted as she watched them both disappear into the house.

She had to go. For Thane's sake. She felt it, like she'd had in the past, that urge that was almost a physical force from the outside pushing her towards the road. She fought it, and took a step towards his cabin. Inside Thane was kicking off his boots. She closed the door behind her and stood there watching him.

"Look, Thane, I wanted to—"

"Save your apology," he said.

"Apology? Why would I apologize?! After what he said?"

"And you said nothing? Like insinuating he doesn't know how to read?" He put up a hand to stop her from responding and with his other hand he rubbed his eyes. "Listen, Grady, I'm beat. All I want to do is sleep."

He pushed Beau off the couch, laid down on his back and put his arms under his head and stared up into the darkness of the high ceiling. He didn't close his eyes. "I'll see you in the morning," he said.

He wouldn't though. That's what Grady had been trying to tell him. She had wanted to thank him. It hadn't been his choice to host her, but he hadn't been unkind. In fact she'd enjoyed her stay more than she ever should have. That's what she had wanted to tell Thane, and that she couldn't stay. It might get him into trouble with the judge who had remanded her to his care. But she had the feeling he'd have a lot less trouble in general without Grady around.

She looked at him for one last time and then walked up the circular stairway to the loft. She lay down in his bed, under his sheets. She did not rest her head on his pillow. She hugged it to her chest and buried her face in it. How quickly she'd gotten used to him. How comfortable she'd been here in an impossible situation. How quickly she'd be gone.

She heard Beau's paws padding up the stairs and she didn't protest when he propped his forelegs on the bed and half-pulled and half-jumped up next to her. She was going to miss him too.

Chapter Seven

Grady hadn't really slept during the night. She was awake when Thane got up. She heard him come up the stairs, pull some clothes out of drawers. She did not open her eyes, but she knew he came to stand next to her, because the room darkened as he passed between her and the window. For a long moment she felt his presence and then his hand brushed her arm as he pulled at Beau's collar and dragged the complaining dog from the bed. She heard both their steps on the stairs. After a few minutes she heard the door close behind them both and she opened her eyes to an empty house.

Grady didn't need to get dressed. She'd slept in her T-shirt and jeans. She grabbed the rest of her things from the dresser next to the bed and once downstairs stuffed everything into her backpack. She wasn't hungry, but she found one of Thane's hiking bottles, filled it with the clear well water and put it inside her backpack and zipped it up. Then she left the house and closed the door behind her.

At the barn she hesitated for a moment and then put all her weight against its door and pushed it open. On top of the toolbox, she found what she was looking for: the rough carving of Beau that Thane had whittled.

"I'm sorry, Thane," she said softly, as she opened her backpack, put in the small sculpture and zipped it up.

She heard a throat clearing and turned to see that she was trapped.

"Where ya goin'?" Dan Hardin asked in his gravelly voice.

"For a walk," Grady said after a pause.

"Don't ya have work to do?" he asked, pointing with his cane at the furniture.

"Not today," Grady said. Not any other day either. "I'll see you later," she lied as she went to the door, but he didn't let her pass.

He squinted at her face and then at her backpack. "Young folks are always in a rush. Rushing into things. And outta things."

"Could you let me by?" Grady said.

"I could. If you'd be so kind as to get an old man a cup of coffee. My machine don't work proper."

Grady sighed as he stepped aside. She put down her backpack and went down to the house. Thane hadn't made any extra coffee, so she had to make a new pot.

When she came back, Dan had taken a seat in one of the Adirondack chairs, his big rubber boots stretched out into the sun that was working its way into the barn. He didn't take the coffee from her, just asked her to set it down next to him. She did and picked up her backpack.

He nodded at the bench across from him. "Why don't you keep me company while I drink this," he said.

But he wasn't drinking it, Grady noticed as she sat down. She fiddled with the garnet on her finger.

"New ring," Dan said.

"Hmm," Grady responded, surprised the old man could even see it.

"I noticed Thane had one too. Pity he didn't think to invite me to the weddin'"

Grady looked up. "Oh, Dan, it wasn't like that. There wasn't anybody there, just the witnesses and the justice. It all happened so quick, and for all the wrong reasons." She paused for a moment and looked at him. "Did Thane tell you we got married?"

"Nope," he said, a smile carving itself into his sunken cheeks. "You just did. And I can't imagine any wrong reasons for getting married," he said. "Especially if you're bringing a baby into this crazy world."

"No! That's not the reason," Grady said quickly.

"Well what's wrong then? Why are you thinking of leaving?"

"Who told you I was leaving?"

"Your backpack. And the look on your face. It's too damn easy to walk away. They oughta put handcuffs on couples nowadays instead of wedding bands."

Grady winced; she'd worn both in less than a week.

He held up his left hand and pointed at the gold ring there. Even from a distance Grady could see how scuffed and dull it was. "No one seems to realize what it's for any more. It ain't a chain. It's like one of those life savers they throw off a ship when you're drowning. It's there to hold you up when you're down."

It was a nice theory he had, but in Grady's case it didn't apply. Hers wasn't a real marriage.

Suddenly he stopped talking and cocked his head to the side as if listening for something. Then he slapped his knees and stood up awkwardly. "Well thanks for the coffee, Grady. I'll see you later."

Dan Hardin walked out of the barn, waved to the driver of the car that pulled up along in front and walked away towards his house. He hadn't touched a drop of his coffee.

Grady picked up her backpack and stepped outside the barn towards the car as Shauna Oplin rolled the passenger's side window down and called to Grady from the driver's side. "Get in," she said without a greeting.

Grady slid the barn door closed, threw her backpack into the backseat and got into the passenger's side. She hardly had a chance to buckle her seatbelt before Shauna backed the car up quickly, turned and took off, spitting gravel against the barn door.

"Did you mean what you said?" Shauna asked as the car bumped along the ruts in the long back road. "That you'd make my husband regret what he did."

Grady couldn't remember saying that. She didn't know what to say and Shauna's frown grew deeper in the silence.

"Jim's already been passed over for promotion twice. The first time when I met him because of the problems with my brother."

"Problems? How is your brother?" Grady asked.

"It's a long story," Shauna sighed. "But all that crap going on cost Jim his promotion. He was up for it again last year, but he he was talking about Bigfoot out there in the woods, and they wouldn't take him seriously."

"Bigfoot? That's probably the guy who set fire to the shed at the cabin! So, he is looking for him."

Shauna took her eyes off the road long enough to give Grady a hard look. "Was! He dropped that stupid theory, but not soon enough to get the promotion. He's been passed over too many times. I don't care about the money, but he needs to get off the road and get behind a desk. He let his guard down with you Grady. I think that's why he's so angry, and why he was embarrassed to admit it to me—he just said he'd had an accident at work. But what will happen next time if it's some drug dealer or a terrorist? The Northway's the only direct route between New York City and Montreal. You wouldn't believe the stuff and the people you'll find on it."

Shauna paused. "What you do to him will affect me too, Grady. We've got two kids, you know. It's not easy to find work here. He's up for sergeant now, but if you press charges or do something crazy, he won't stand a chance."

"Shauna, I wouldn't do that! You know me."

She glanced at Grady before she pulled out onto the smoother Route 9 heading south. "I thought I knew you. But, Grady, what I saw last night—" Her voice trailed off.

"Shauna, I swear to you, I would never do anything to hurt you ... or your family."

"I want to believe that Grady, I really do, but I don't know."

"I wish there was something I could do to show you that I haven't changed."

Shauna smiled suddenly. "I was hoping you'd say that. Actually there is something you can do for me. And you will change." She looked over again, but she wasn't looking at Grady's face, but her hair, as if sizing it up. "I've got the practical part of my beautician's exam today and Jim's aunt chickened out of being my subject. You're going to fill in for her."

"I'll do anything you ask," Grady said quickly.

"I'm not asking," Shauna said as she pulled onto the Northway towards Glens Falls and accelerated.

Thane dumped a heavy pack of shingles onto the steep roof of the Garnet Lake Episcopal church, and climbed back down the aluminum ladder. Cal was supposed to be helping him, but he was out bidding on new jobs.

Thane picked up the hem of his T-Shirt and used it to wipe the sweat off his face. He was about to heft another pack of shingles onto his shoulder when Shauna Oplin's car pulled into the lot.

She left it running and came over to him. "You got a minute, Thane?"

"I've got to get this finished by tomorrow, before it rains," he said.

She continued anyway. "Grady's not a bad person."

"I know that," he said grudgingly. But she was a difficult person.

"Her parents didn't belong together. They had nothing in common. They fought a lot in the beginning until they kind of started living separate lives. I remember fishing with Grady off the dock one time while her parents were having a big blow-out inside the cabin. We must have been 10 or 11. I was freaked out, but Grady acted like nothing was going on. But I'll never forget the way she looked out over the water like she was looking for something. My aunt called me back for lunch, and I remember Grady saying she was going to take a walk."

Thane sighed, took off his work gloves and rubbed his forehead.

"Everyone's got issues, Shauna. If you're trying to make me feel sorry for her—"

"I'm trying to make you understand. She's going for another walk."

Thane shrugged. "It'll probably do her good."

"That time, she was halfway to the Canadian border before some trucker picked her up and dropped her at the State Trooper barracks in Hamilton County. She's going to run again, Thane. She had that look."

"How far could she get?"

"Pretty far. I guilted her into coming to Glens Falls with me for my exam today. We stopped for lunch afterwards at the diner down there and she bummed 50 bucks off me."

"So?"

"That's next door to the bus depot. She told me she had some shopping to do in town, and she'd take the bus back. I believe she's going to take the bus, but I don't think she plans on getting out in Garnet Lake."

"She'd be a fool to do that. She'd be jumping bail."

"She's not thinking that far ahead right now."

"Why don't you tell Jim?"

Shauna laughed. "The less they see of each other the better. They're too much alike. She's not a bad person," Shauna said again. "She's just going through a tough time."

"And she's putting me through a tough time, too."

"Thane, she's my friend, you've got to help her. And aren't you responsible for her?"

"I'll think about it," he said.

Shauna pulled a folded piece of paper from her back pocket. "Well think fast. Here's the bus schedule. It's due in Garnet Lake in front of the post office in 15 minutes."

"Why don't you get her off the bus?"

"I'm late picking up the boys, and besides, what am I going to do, put a gun to her head?" She opened her car door. "You seem to be able to handle her," she said as she closed the door and pulled away.

He'd heard that before. He didn't like the way it sounded any better the second time around.

Thane pulled in front of the post office in Garnet Lake, in front of the idling Adirondack Trailways bus and left his engine running. The driver had his hand on the lever about to close the door, when Thane jumped up and strode past him.

"You have a ticket, son?"

"Don't need one," Thane said over his shoulder.

He passed Grady by at first. Then he recognized her backpack in the overhead rack and pulled it down. He knew her graceful fingers, and the now-familiar garnet ring that she was twisting around and around on her finger. But she looked so different.

"Let's go," he said gruffly.

She stopped turning the ring and looked up. Her hair was very short, and it framed her face in layered jags, drawing all the attention to her features. She was all eyes and high cheekbones and full lips. Those eyes grew even wider as she recognized him.

"What are you doing here?" she asked.

"I could ask you the same question."

"It's better this way, Thane," she began.

"I'm not here to argue, Grady. Get off this bus or I'll pick up up and carry you off."

"You wouldn't do that!"

"Wouldn't I?"

An elderly woman craned her head around the high seat in front of them. "Do you want me to call the police, honey?" she said.

"Please do," Thane responded.

"No!" Grady said almost at the same time.

Thane took a step back to give Grady room to get out. He followed her to the front of the bus, where the driver let her pass, but put an arm out to block Thane's way.

"Who the hell do you think you are?" the driver asked him.

"I'm her husband," Thane said, stalking past him. At his truck, he threw Grady's backpack into the bed, then went around and opened the passenger side door for her and waited for her to get in. He was not going to say please this time. She looked at him for a moment, then dropped her eyes and got into the truck. Thane slammed the door. Hard. Then he walked around to his side and got in. He sat for a minute before the bus honked its horn, then he pulled out onto Route 9.

"Judge Mullens can't do anything to you," Grady said after awhile. "Remanding me to your care instead of sending me to jail probably isn't legal anyway."

"He gave me a responsibility," Thane said tightly.

"A responsibility," she repeated. He thought he heard a note of bitterness in her voice.

"This isn't about the judge, Grady. Did you ever give me a thought?"

"But I was doing this for you. You'd be better off without me."

"Would I? What about the rustic furniture competition?" He looked over at her briefly. "You made a promise to help me. I need you, Grady."

She turned her face to look out the passenger's side window. "Need," she repeated sullenly as if it were a bad word.

"With your help, I think I can win, or at least place in this competition. And do you know what that means? It means I could get my name out there. I am just a tax bill away from having to pack up and move back to the city. I've got to start making real money instead of working for free to save the cash I lent to Cal. I'll have to find a job and a place to live downstate and then come back when I can on long weekends." He hit the steering wheel with his palm. "Damn it! That's not the way I want to live."

"I'll give you the money," Grady said.

They had reached his barn, and Thane stopped shorter than he needed to.

"You don't get it, do you? I won't take what I don't earn. I can't live like that either."

He killed the engine and sat looking at her. She looked back for a moment, then looked away, pushed Beau aside and got out. Thane stepped out of the truck, and as she came around to pass him on her way to the house, he put a hand on her arm to stop her.

"Wrong way," he said, as he pulled her to the bed of the truck and let her go to grab her backpack. "You want to get away? Then let's go. You have water in here?" he asked her.

She nodded and he unzipped the backpack and dumped its contents out into the bed of the truck on top of his tools. He recognized the high-quality Nalgene bottle for hiking. It was his. He shook his head as he stuffed it back into the now-empty backpack.

"I was going to send it back to you," she said.

"And this?" He picked out a wooden figure of a dog he had carved.

"That I was going to keep."

Thane wondered if it was to remember Beau or himself. Beau,

probably, he thought and it made him even angrier. He tossed it back into the bed of the truck.

"Let's go," he said and took a step towards the path leading away from the barn and into the woods.

"Go where?" she asked.

"Up Ethan Ridge."

"Now?"

"You don't want to?"

"No, it's not that, but do we have time?"

"If we go now. Once the sun goes over the ridge, we'll be feeling our way home."

"I'm not afraid of the dark."

He looked down at her thoughtfully. "I know. You're not afraid of anything. Or anyone. That's the problem," he said.

"My problem?!"

"Grady, we can argue all you want, but let's do it when we get to the top." He turned back to the path then, but not before grabbing her hand and pulling her after him. She stumbled to catch up, but he didn't let her go. She wanted to run, didn't she? He was more than happy to let her have her way.

Grady had to put all her energy and concentration into her feet, to keep her balance as Thane pulled her along behind him up the trail to Ethan Ridge. She'd assumed he'd let her go as soon as they got started. But he didn't. Either he was afraid she'd bolt again, or he was punishing her for running away. Maybe both. It was all she could do to keep up, she had no energy to waste on thinking. One after the other, like ballast, she had to drop the anger, the frustration, the doubt.

Thane reached the outcropping of bald rock at the top of the ridge a split second before she did and they both sank down onto its mossy surface, breathing hard. He let go of her hand, took the backpack off his shoulders and reached in for his water bottle and handed it to her. He watched her as she drank so quickly it spilled down the side of her mouth. She handed the bottle back to him, but he didn't drink at first, just kept looking at her, almost as if he were deciding whether he was still angry with her. His eyes flicked from her face to her cropped hair and she ran her hands self-consciously through it.

"It's awful, isn't it?" she said.

"You're beautiful," he said.

Grady looked away. "You don't have to lie to make me feel better. I deserved what Shauna did to me."

He caught her under the chin and lifted her face so she had to look at him. "I mean what I say, Grady," he said. "You should know that by now."

His voice was hard, but his touch was gentle. She searched his eyes and couldn't find the anger she'd seen when he'd pulled her off the bus. She found instead something she couldn't exactly name. She would have looked longer, but Beau pushed his way between them and Thane let her go.

She looked away to the forest below them. Its waves of rich brown, burgundy and green fanned out unevenly to the horizon. Garnet Lake was a drop of spilled mercury caught between two peaks.

The air was so crisp and fresh, she thought she could taste it. The peak was a lonely place, so far removed from the world, but not for her, sitting here, next to Thane. In the cool breeze winding up the bald rock, she felt the warmth of him. She had wanted to run so badly, but she realized now, more than anything, she had wanted to be found.

The sun was getting close to the horizon, seeming to set it on fire and turn the clouds amber. They would have to go soon, but she wanted to stay here forever. She'd always had a problem leaving these woods.

She could see Thane's house from here. She looked away to the east to avoid having to see the bare spot across the lake where her father's cabin used to be. Her eyes caught on a wide gash in the thick woods. She gasped and leaned forward.

"You can see Hoffman's mine from here," she said. She glanced up at the horizon. "I bet if we waited 'til twilight, we'd see smoke. Or better yet, if we stayed 'til it got dark, we could probably make out the guy's campfire."

"What guy, Grady?"

"The one responsible for all those burglaries and the vandalism, who set fire to the shed at my Dad's cabin. There's an old rail line leading into the mine," she said with determination. "Most of that's been salvaged for scrap metal, but the path is still there. And there's a ton of logging roads in and out. It makes it a perfect place to have a hideout."

Thane sighed. "Grady, let it go."

"I can't! It's personal. My Dad and I spent so much time back there, hammering away at those rocks. It was like a fairy tale; the whole place sparkled like rubies. I found a garnet once the size of my thumb. I felt like the richest girl in the world."

She turned to him suddenly to find he was watching her. "You think I'm crazy, don't you?" she said.

"You have no idea what I'm thinking." Something about his voice, about the intensity of his gaze made her shiver. He looked away to the horizon as if checking nature's clock. The sun was closing in on it.

She wanted to ask him what he was thinking, but he didn't give her a chance.

"We better go," he said and his voice was different now. "You're cold and we don't have much daylight left."

He took her hand and pulled her up. "Do you still feel like running?" he asked.

She shook her head and his grip tightened as if he weren't satisfied with that answer.

"Promise me you'll stay, Grady." he said.

Her heart answered with a yes, before she could even speak. This was where she wanted to be. Where she wanted to belong. And she wanted to belong to Thane.

But her heart hadn't waited for Thane to finish his sentence.

"Until the Rustic Furniture competition is over."

He didn't want her here forever.

"Promise me," he said again when she didn't answer.

She looked down at her hand in his. "I promise," she said. But her heart had made a different promise. One that he would never keep.

Thane let her go and turned to head down the ridge with Beau close behind him. Grady looked back one more time to the horizon that was dimming.

"What are you waiting for?" he called to her from the path.

For something that was never going to happen, she thought. And then she turned to follow him.

Chapter Eight

The next day Grady was on her way to the barn when the phone rang. Thane was already out working with Cal. She didn't pick it up, until she heard Shauna's voice on the answering machine.

"I wanted to let you know that I passed my beautician's exam, Grady!" Shauna said. "They loved what I did to your hair. I got the highest marks in the whole class."

"I'm glad," Grady said as she ran her hand through her shorn locks.

"We're going out tonight to celebrate."

"Thane said he'd be working late, I don't know if we could make it," Grady said slowly.

"Oh my gosh, no, Grady, I wasn't inviting you. I didn't mean all of us. Listen, no one is going to tell me who I can associate with, especially not my husband, but until he gets this promotion, I think it's best that we don't get together." She added into the awkward silence. "I'm sorry, Grady, but you're not good for him."

He wasn't the only one she wasn't good for. "No, it's okay, Shauna, I understand, I really do. When is he up for promotion?"

"In a few weeks. Then we'll catch up. I'm so excited you're here. I've got big plans for us."

Grady had no plan except to be gone in three weeks when her trust came through and she made bail.

"I'll see you soon, okay, Grady," Shauna said into the silence.

Grady didn't know what to say. But Shauna was already saying goodbye, and Grady was left with nothing but the dial tone in her ear.

Cal had hired a laborer and between him and Thane, they'd finished the roof of the episcopal church by early afternoon the next day.

Thane pulled up in front of his barn. Dan Hardin was standing just inside the entrance like he was standing guard. He nodded curtly as Thane came to stand next to him.

"Don't even bother trying to talk to her, she's worse than you when she's working."

Grady sat, one leg under her, leaning into the headboard of the bed at an odd angle. He couldn't see what she'd done, but he could see most of it was still untouched. He felt a small jab of disappointment. And then he felt a hard jab from Dan Hardin's cane on the side of his boot. Even through the leather, it stung, and he turned to the old man.

"You're welcome, by the way," Dan said.

"What the hell do you mean?" Thane asked.

"I'd like to know what you mean, chasing a girl like this away. What'd you say to her to make her wanna run? I kept her here as long as I could yesterday morning. But just remember I ain't a babysitter and I ain't your damned marriage counselor."

"It wasn't my fault."

"Well I hope you apologized."

"Dan, you better get your hearing checked. I told you I didn't do anything wrong."

"You better check your attitude, boy. I heard you just fine. It don't matter whose fault it is. 'I'm sorry,' are the most important words you'll ever say in a marriage."

Thane sighed. Dan Hardin had no idea what was really going on. And yet he'd been smart enough to realize Thane and Grady had gotten married. The man wasn't a fool, but he needed to mind his own business. Thane changed the subject. "I'm heading down to Glens Falls soon, maybe tomorrow, if you need anything," he said.

Dan pulled a wrinkled piece of paper out of the bib of his overalls with thick fingers. "Never thought you'd ask," he said.

"Never thought you'd say please or thank you either," Thane said to himself as the old man shuffled away up the road.

"Same to you," Dan grunted over his shoulder.

Thane shook his head, then stepped over to where Grady was working. She had clipped her bangs back on one side, but the rest of her short hair came forward to frame her face. He didn't realize he had stopped watching her work and had been studying her profile, until she turned to the toolbox next to him and noticed him finally, and the way he was staring.

"Hi," she said. She made a self-conscious motion to smooth her hair back from her shoulder, but seemed surprised when her hand met nothing.

"What do you think?" she nodded at the headboard.

"It's the view from the ridge." Thane said.

"I could do something else, it's not too late."

"No, it's perfect."

She looked up at him and smiled doubtfully. She shook her hand a few times, rubbing it carefully with her left and then picked up the awl again.

"You're working too hard," Thane said.

She shook her head. "Just with the wrong tools, maybe."

"I can pick something up when I go to Glens Falls."

"I'll just go with you," she said. "It would be easier than trying to explain what I need."

"That won't be necessary," he said. "I'll buy a couple things and what you don't use I can return."

She cocked her head and her eyes darkened.

"You don't want me leaving the property and getting into trouble do you?" she asked.

Thane took a deep breath, giving himself a moment to come up with a diplomatic way to agree with her, but she shrugged.

"You're not the only one," he thought he heard her say under her breath and then louder: "It's okay, I don't want to leave here anyway. I was hoping to pick up some clothes though. All I brought with me were jeans and T-shirts. I just thought I'd be here a couple days to open up the cabin." She paused for a moment as if just remembering it wasn't there. "Anyway, I wanted to pick up a swimsuit and I wouldn't mind looking presentable for the competition." She shrugged again. "I guess it doesn't matter. The water's too cold yet anyway ... and you don't need me at the furniture competition."

"Of course I need you," Thane said.

She looked at him with a doubtful expression as if searching for something in his eyes that she wasn't sure she'd find. She bent her head towards her work again, and Thane could see her wince as she put pressure on the awl.

He picked up her hand, and she gasped.

"It's just a blister," she said through clenched teeth.

"Grady, this is more than a blister, you need to take a break."

"I can't waste any time. You only have less than a week and a half 'til the competition."

"We'll make it. I'm serious, I'll lock the barn if I have to. Take a break."

She stood up. "I can update your website instead, I guess," she said.

"I don't have one."

"Then I'll make one, that's what I did at the insurance company."

"I have a better idea," Thane said.

"What?"

"You'll see."

It had been a long time since Thane had put the old aluminum row boat into the water. He threw two long-unused fishing poles into it and added two musty life vests, just in case it had sprung any leaks since he last used it.

Grady had rolled up her jeans, put on one of his old paint-specked baseball caps and with her short hair, it should have made her look boyish, but those big eyes and the angles of her face would never let him mistake her for a boy.

"Let me row, too," Grady said as Thane helped her in, and he pulled away from the dock.

"So you can have blisters in different places? We're supposed to be out here to give your hands a rest."

He rowed until he reached the deepest part of the lake, where the water was clear and cold, and he put the oars away and reached for his fishing pole. Grady was already casting gracefully like she was throwing a sliver of sunshine into the lake.

"If you get bored, let me know," he said.

She laughed and angled her head to look up at him under the visor of his old cap.

"I won't get bored, trust me. Fishing is one of those things either you get or you don't. I think that's the thing my parents fought about the most. My Mom would want to know exactly when my Dad would be back from fishing." She shook her head. "But you know how it is. There's always one more out there."

He nodded.

"I don't want it to sound like my Dad was lazy. He worked hard, too hard, and he needed this. He needed to go hunting with his buddies when he and I came up on weekends."

"He'd leave you alone?"

"I never thought of it as alone. I was never afraid by myself. Not up here. Besides I hardly noticed he was gone. He'd leave at some awful hour in the morning long before I was awake, and be back in time for lunch. I have no idea, really, who most of his friends were." She laughed, but there was a little sadness in it. "They all had stupid nicknames, like Skidder, or Moose."

"Moose?" Thane sat up a little straighter.

"You know him?" she asked, her voice hopeful.

Thane shook his head. Couldn't be. He'd thought he'd heard Judge Mullens referred to as Moose, but hunters didn't have to be an original bunch, it was probably a common nickname. Besides at the arraignment, Mullens had made no sign that he knew Grady.

"You never hunted?" Thane asked.

She shrugged. "My Dad taught me how to shoot, but hunting was his thing. I'd rather fish. There's something so peaceful about it. And besides when you catch a fish, you can still let it go. When you hunt something, when you shoot it, it's gone forever."

She stopped talking and he looked up. Her eyes had gone wide and he glanced over his shoulder to see what she was seeing. There wasn't much left of her father's cabin to see. It was like a house of cards that had fallen in on itself. Thane cursed. They'd been drifting, but he hadn't given much thought to the direction.

"I want to go home," Grady said.

He picked up the oars, placed them in their moorings, as she bent her head and put the heel of her hands to her eyes. "Please, just take me back home, please take me home."

He turned the boat with one oar until her back was to the demolished cabin.

"You can open your eyes now," he said, but she didn't until they reached his dock.

She started to get out even before he'd had a chance to moor the boat, and she tumbled onto the dock on her knees and pulled herself up.

She turned to him and her face was white. "Tell Cal to get rid of it. Haul everything out to the dump. Anything that's left, just bury it." She turned suddenly, stumbled over the lip of the dock into the grass, got up again and dropped to all fours. Thane tied the boat quickly to the dock and went to her.

"There's nothing left," she said.

But Thane suddenly remembered that wasn't exactly true.

Grady had known all this time the cabin wasn't standing, but she hadn't really accepted it until now. She wished she hadn't told Cal to halt all work there. It would have been better if it had all been wiped away and she could still have her memories of what it used to be. Now she could never see it whole again.

Thane put a hand on her arm. "I need to show you something,"

"I don't want to see any more," she said, but he pulled her up gently and led her up the steep path, past his house, across the drive and to the barn. In one of the back stalls he pulled a box out from beneath a rickety table.

"I found this at your cabin. It was protected under a section of the wall. It was the only thing that wasn't ruined in the rain."

She sank to her knees and opened it carefully as if she were afraid something might jump out.

There was a brass statue of a fish, from when she'd won third place in the Garnet Lake Fishing Derby, a collection of snail shells, nothing of value, yet everything priceless and full of memories. She pulled out a framed photo: her father stood with an arm around Grady as she struggled to hold up the largest rainbow perch she'd ever caught. She wiped the glass carefully, even though there was no dust on it, and put it gently on the floor of the barn and after a long pause started rummaging through the box again.

"Look at this," she said. "Remember I told you I found a garnet as big as my thumb? Well, my thumb must have been a lot smaller back then. This is it."

She held the rough stone up into a shaft of shy sunlight, and admired its dark red glow.

"I always wanted to get a necklace made out of it, just something simple. There's a jeweler in Glens Falls, isn't there? Could you take it with you, and see if they could polish or cut it and put it in a setting?"

He put his hand out and she dropped the garnet into it.

"But, what kind of a setting?" he asked. " I wouldn't know what to tell them."

She looked down at her hands, but couldn't think of anything. She unconsciously twirled her ring around which had become a habit.

"Here!" She pulled her ring off and put it into his palm and it disappeared as he closed his hand around it. "Something to match this. I don't care what it costs."

Her ring finger felt bare. She unconsciously rubbed the spot where it was missing.

Then she started putting the items back in the box.

The picture was last. "He didn't tell me," she said quietly, rubbing her thumb over her father's picture.

"What?"

"My Dad. He didn't tell me how sick he was. I should have known, I guess. He asked me if I could get away to the cabin, take off the whole week around the Columbus day holiday. He seemed tired, kind of thoughtful. I thought he just needed a break and I was glad he was taking it. We spent a lot of time fishing. We didn't talk a lot. We never really did. We understood each other. Or at least I thought we did.

"Anyway, we were supposed to come back the last week in October to shut off the water and drain the pipes before winter."

"What happened?" Thane said after she was quiet for too long.

"He collapsed a few days before Halloween. The cancer had been eating away at him, but it was his heart that gave out. He lasted about a week, but it was too late by then to say goodbye."

"I'm sorry, Grady," Thane said. "I can only imagine what it's like to lose someone you love."

"I hate him!" Grady said as she threw the framed photo into the box, and turned her hands to fists. "I'm so angry with him. He knew for months how sick he was and he didn't tell me. I hate him for it."

She looked down at her fists. Thane didn't tell her she was wrong. He took her hand instead and pried open her fingers one by one and then entwined his own in hers. She couldn't form a fist again no matter how she tried.

The next day Thane left for Glens Falls early before Grady was up. It took him all day to pick up his supplies, plus fill the long list Dan Hardin had given him and to wander around the mall looking for stuff for Grady.

His last stop was the jeweler. He showed them the rough garnet, and the setting on Grady's wedding ring that had come from the town hall's lost and found box. They asked if they could keep it to work from. Thane hadn't expected his own reaction. He'd told them no, and insisted they make a copy somehow, or a sketch or take a picture. It belonged on Grady's finger.

The saleswoman disappeared into a back room and came out a few minutes later with the garnet ring, which she laid on the counter.

"You can have it resized," she said.

"The garnet? No, it fits her perfectly."

She smiled. "I meant yours."

He looked down to realize he'd been fidgeting with his own

wedding ring.

"It's borrowed," he said.

"Here let me get a size for you," she said slipping a measuring band around his finger. "We've got a nice selection," she added jotting a number down on the paperwork for Grady's necklace.

"This is only temporary," Thane said.

"Because you have to give it back?"

"No, I'm not talking about the ring. I'm talking about the marriage."

She looked at him for a moment with a smile that was less friendly, then shrugged, her hand half-way to the case holding the shining gold bands. "Well, if you want to make it permanent, you know where we are."

And where would Grady be when she came into her money and made bail? Gone, and Thane wouldn't even have a ring to remember her by.

Thane came back from Glens Falls and pulled in front of the open barn doors. He got out of his truck, hefted a bag of tools from the bed and dropped it into the corner of the barn and went to see what Grady had been up to. It was just getting towards dusk, but the barn had darkened already. A cabin, her father's cabin was taking shape on the headboard in the forefront and Ethan ridge spread out above it in the background.

He crouched down next to her. "It looks good," he said softly.

Grady turned to him with a serious expression, her mouth a firm line of concentration, then she blinked and gave him a welcoming smile that didn't fade instantly like it did in her first days with him. "Oh," she said. "You're back already?"

"Already? I've been gone all day."

"Oh," she said again. "I can stop in a minute."

"You can stop now," he said noticing how she'd bandaged up the blisters on her right hand. "Please," he added.

She hesitated then put down the awl she was working with. "Ok," she said. "Were they able to do anything with that garnet, at the jeweler?"

"They can't tell 'til they cut it and polish it, but they thought it would be enough to make a necklace. They took a picture of the ring setting, so they didn't have to keep it. Here."

He was crouched down on one knee and he had to lean back slightly to pull the ring out from his jeans pocket. He could have just handed it to her. Instead he picked up her left hand and slipped the ring over her finger. He stared down at it for a moment. Could it only have been a little more than a week since he'd slipped the ring on her finger at the municipal center during their hasty marriage vows? He turned the ring so it was just right, surprised again how well it fit her, like it had always belonged there. He looked up to find her watching him. The light was behind her, and her wide almond-shaped eyes were dark and he couldn't read them. Her lips were parted as if she wanted to say something.

Their ceremony hadn't exactly been complete. The judge had never asked him to kiss the bride. He could make it complete now, if he wanted. But what would he be starting? He was already tangled up. He reminded himself that Grady was too unpredictable, that she'd cost him one friendship already. But right now on one knee, holding Grady's hand in his, being tangled up didn't seem like a bad thing. If he wanted to, he could pull her closer. He wanted to. The question was, should he?

If Beau hadn't nosed his way between them, he might have answered the question. Thane should have thanked him, he was saving him from himself. But Thane wasn't feeling very thankful.

The next morning Thane was up and out of the house early and at Cal's office making changes to the Blackburn plans. The Blackburns had 'as good as' approved them, and since Cal had hired a crew based on his optimism, it freed Thane up to come home after lunch.

He expected to find Grady working in the barn as usual, but she wasn't there, even though the barn door hung open.

He heard a splash and made his way down the steep walk past his house and out to the edge of the aluminum dock and crouched down. Beau, rooting in the weeds at the swampy end of the shore noticed Thane first and barked. Grady waved to him then from the water and swam over to the dock.

"No wonder you're a good carpenter," Grady said as she treaded water.

"What do you mean?"

"You can measure with your eyes. Everything you bought me fits perfectly, even the swimsuit." She shook her head. "I have to try on about ten before I find one that fits."

Thane shrugged. He didn't want to admit that he'd spent enough time observing her to know her curves.

"I don't want you swimming when I'm not here," he said

She smiled. She was close enough now to reach up and put a hand on the dock, but did not make a move to come out of the water. "You sound just like my Dad."

"I bet you didn't listen to him either."

"Actually I did, but that's because we didn't have a dog. Beau would save me, wouldn't you buddy? And I'm sure you know CPR."

At the sound of his name Beau stopped digging in the reeds and looked up.

"That's the thing, I don't know CPR, and Beau is no hero," Thane said. "Trust me."

"Yes you are, Beau, aren't you?" Grady said. "You'd save me, right? Yes you would," she went on in a sing-song voice.

As if he wanted to prove himself, Beau came trotting over to jump into the water, and landed on top of her. His weight pushed her under, and she came up spluttering as Beau put his paws against her and pushed her under again.

Thane didn't think about how he was dressed, certainly not for swimming in his work jeans and grey T-shirt. He jumped in, came up for air, pushed Beau away and put his arm around Grady's back. He let go of Beau just long enough to grab one of the dock's supports, and his arm acted like a barrier. He pulled Grady up, and the motion brought her naturally against him. And her arms went instinctively around his neck as she coughed.

"Oh my gosh," she said between gasps. "You were right."

Her wet hair clung to her flushed face. The sun had drawn freckles on her pretty nose and her eyes and the water reflected its sparkle. She stopped sputtering and quieted as she clung to him.

"This is becoming a habit for you," she said when she got her breath back.

"What do you mean?" he asked.

"Saving my life."

Right now, holding her tightly against him, the water rocking them gently, the trees guarding them along the shore, saving her was the last thing on his mind. In fact he wasn't thinking at all, not this close to her. He forgot everything, how they met, how she could be. He forgot Beau until the dog pushed his way between them, whining. Thane became suddenly aware of how cold the water was. He made sure Grady had a hold of the dock and then he grabbed Beau by the collar and pulled the dog towards and up onto shore. Thane sat on the bulkhead and worked on untying his soaked boots, as he watched Grady pull herself up onto the dock. They'd known each other a little over a week. He wanted to know her better, every part of her.

He shook his head. He had to get himself together. He'd gone literally jumping off the deep end seeing her in trouble. He didn't need to get himself in deeper.

Thane took his job seriously, Grady thought, feeling suddenly cold as she climbed out of the water. The judge had remanded her to Thane's care and he had his hands full making sure she didn't run, making sure she didn't drown. He must feel like a warden and a lifeguard rolled into one. She was surprised he left her alone at all. As she pushed her wet hair back out of her face and reached for the towel she'd thrown on the grass, she noticed the way his eyes narrowed as if waiting for the next crazy thing she'd do. The tenseness in his clenched jaw told her he was on guard. He shook his head, and she looked away not wanting to see the disappointment on his face. He had seen her at her worst, and he would always expect that in her.

Thane spent the next few days out in the woods searching for the right branch, or twisted root to incorporate into a rustic chair. Honestly, he was avoiding Grady, but today the heat of the past few days had given way to thunderstorms and he was in the barn trying to assemble the chair. There was no pattern he could follow, the objects he worked with dictated their own style and it took all his concentration to make something functional out of something natural.

Thunder echoed off the ridge and he walked over to close the barn door to find Grady standing at the entrance watching the lake which had turned into a small ocean with churning white caps.

He stood there with her as the rain ricocheted against the dirt drive and the thunder seemed to crack against the barn walls. Grady had been using an old drop cloth as a cushion beneath her as she worked at odd angles on the headboard of the rustic bed, and Beau crawled under it now whimpering and shivering, making the old blanket seem to come alive like a ghost.

Thane was watching Grady's profile and when lightning hit the center of the lake, he saw it reflected in her eyes. She didn't flinch as the thunder shook the ground just a moment later.

Thane put a hand on her arm and pulled her back a step. She looked down at his hand and when she looked up again her eyes had soaked in the darkness of the barn.

"I know it's hard for you to have me here," she said.

"I never said that."

"You don't have to. I can tell the way you act. This wasn't your choice, I don't blame you."

He turned her towards him. "It's not you, it's me, Grady," he lied. "The judge sentenced you to my care, not to hard labor. I shouldn't be making you work. I feel bad about it."

"But I'm glad to."

"I know. That just makes it worse."

"But, I owe you."

"I owe you."

She put out a hand. "Why don't we call it even?"

The storm was spending itself, disappearing over the ridge and leaving an unnatural calm, but the light against the mountains was an eerie yellow, the air was still full of prickling electricity.

"And I'll promise not to get into any more trouble," she said. He took her hand and held it longer than he needed to, resisting the urge to pull her in closer. The storm would circle around again, he was sure.

Chapter Nine

A week later, Grady lay on her stomach, propped up on rough blankets, painstakingly adding touches here and there on the mountain scene she had etched into the bark of the headboard of the bed frame Thane had constructed.

There wasn't much left to do, the competition was tomorrow, but she couldn't stop. That would mean it was over, this temporary partnership with Thane.

It hadn't been all work. They'd been back up to the ridge three more times when Grady needed inspiration and for Thane to collect more wood and pine cones and all the natural material the forest contributed to his rustic furniture. They'd been out fishing again too all over Garnet Lake, avoiding only the small bay where her father's cabin used to be.

After the last bad storm, the weather had been dry and pleasant, the sky filled with soft, slow-moving clouds. But over the last two days the heat had started to thicken again, and the only thing that could break it was another storm. It was coming, Grady could feel it. She just hoped it held off until after the rustic furniture fair was over. The lake was smooth, the sky still, but it seemed like an unnatural calm.

Like her stay here with Thane? Since the run-in Grady had had with Jim Oplin at The Well, Thane had done everything he could to keep her away from his friend or anyone else, except his neighbor Dan Hardin, who wouldn't have adhered to any rules anyway. Thane had done the food shopping, picked up supplies. It was an unspoken agreement that she couldn't leave this place. And she hadn't wanted to.

She and Thane had settled into a routine. He seemed to have finally relaxed around her, though she would catch him from time to time watching her carefully as if he still expected another outburst. But for the most part they worked together well. They knew, too, how to be quiet around each other. Grady wished it could go on and on, but

Thane had asked her to stay only until the competition was over tomorrow. They'd never talked about the future. Why should they have?

In another week, the waiting period would be over and she'd come into her trust and could make bail. She would be free to go anywhere. The problem was, she didn't want to go anywhere. She didn't want to be free.

She hadn't been aware of Thane standing next to her and she jumped at the sound of his voice. "Let's call it a day," he said quietly. "In fact, I think it's after midnight. Let's call it tomorrow. We've got an early start, it's going to take us a couple hours to unload and set up at the show."

She glanced over her shoulder for just a moment before turning her eyes back to her work. The light from the construction lamp he'd set up for her made a giant of his shadow against the barn board.

"I'm almost done," she said.

"That's what you said yesterday."

"Just give me a few more minutes."

"That's what you said a few hours ago." He waited another moment. "You're not going to stop, unless I make you, are you?" He pulled the etching tool from Grady's hand and tossed it into his open toolbox.

While she protested, he walked over to the barn door and pushed it open as far as it would go.

"I want to show you something," he said, as he came back to her and switched off the bright light.

"I can't see a thing," she said.

"You're looking in the wrong direction. Turn over," he said as he stretched out next to her on the slatted bed frame.

By turning the light off, he had switched the sky on. The open barn door was like a curtain pulled aside for a celestial show. And closer to earth the fireflies blinked on and off, like tiny spotlights. The woods were a busy orchestra pit of crickets. They must have been tuning up all night, but she only noticed them now.

"You're so lucky to have all this," Grady said softly after a long time.

"I'll be lucky if I don't lose it."

"I won't let you lose it."

She felt him stiffen.

"I won't be indebted to you."

Grady nudged him with an elbow. "You already are. Do you know how much my artwork costs?"

"I have no idea. How much?"

"How would I know? No one's ever paid me for it. I'll take room and board for the next week until I make bail."

He had relaxed, but she sensed a tenseness in him again.

She searched the sky for a constellation she could recognize. It was all a beautiful pattern, that didn't make sense to her. Did she fit in?

"Do you believe in life after death?" she said after awhile.

"I haven't thought about it much. I've been too busy trying to figure out how to make a living."

"All those stars can't be for nothing. Can they? When someone dies, it just seems wrong that the world doesn't skip a beat, that there's no sign they made it to the other side or wherever they're supposed to go."

Just then a star seemed to tumble out of the sky, leaving a brief spark behind it as it disappeared forever. Grady gasped and raised herself up and turned to Thane. She could barely make out the lines of his face, the deep dark orbs of his eyes. "Did you see that?" she whispered. He didn't answer except to pull her in against him. She clung to him, her eyes closed tightly, trying to hold to that image of the falling star. She didn't need to see the light to know it was all around them.

Chapter Ten

Thane was awake to see the dawn crowding through the open barn doors. His arm was dead asleep. He didn't want to disturb Grady's head which rested on it. She lay on her side, face towards him. Thane didn't move, except for his eyes which caressed the fine lines of her face, her delicate nose and cheekbones. It was a pretty face, a beautiful face. A strand of her dark hair had fallen across her cheek and he resisted the urge to push it gently behind her ear. He didn't want to wake her. She hadn't said another word last night after that shooting star, but she'd held onto him like he was a lifeline and she was lost on the water. And he'd held her as tightly as he could until she finally relaxed against him, and a long time after that she fell asleep. Sometime in the night he'd pulled the scratchy old wool blanket around them, and it was twisted between them now. Thane didn't think he'd slept at all.

A crow exploded the stillness with a shriek and Grady's eyes flew open. They widened in surprise as her body tensed and then she relaxed as she seemed to get her bearings. She closed her eyes again and stretched slightly against him. Into him.

"Morning," she mumbled as her eyes fluttered open again and she sighed. "I haven't slept out in so long, I forgot how the fresh air knocks me out."

She turned her head even more to face him. "Guess you'll have to sell this bed as used now," she said.

Thane didn't respond, he watched the smile brighten her eyes, just as the world was waking up outside the barn. She was so close, so warm. His eyes dropped to her lips and the smile on them faded, but not into a frown, they parted as if she wanted to say something, as she tilted her head towards him.

Suddenly a siren went off and it seemed to drive something physical between them and they both sat up. The siren flared again, then was replaced by the sound of tires eating up and spitting out the gravel of Thane's long driveway.

By the time Jim Oplin pulled up to the barn doors, Thane and Grady were standing at the entrance.

"Working early?" he said as he got out of the cruiser and straightened the creases in his uniform, tugging the hem of his jacket straight. His eyes moved over Grady's disheveled hair, her wrinkled shirt. "Or would you call it working late, or what would you call it?"

"What are doing here, Opie?" Thane asked.

"I told you I'd help you load up, didn't I, for this furniture thing?" he said.

That was before all this stuff had come between them. Before Grady Henderson had come between them. "Or am I wrong?" Opie continued.

"No, you're right. Thanks. I appreciate it."

"What are friends for?" Thane couldn't miss the sarcasm in it as his friend came around to the pickup with its trailer and seemed to measure it with his eyes. "What time are you coming back?" Opie asked.

"I don't know. Probably late. Evening sometime, why?"

"Oh," he said and there was silence.

"Why's that?"

He shrugged. "You better sell all this crap, 'cause I won't be here to help you unload. I got work to do."

"Overtime?" Thane asked.

Opie opened his mouth, then looked at Grady and it closed in a tight line, and he shook his head.

"Looks like you two are working overtime, though," Opie said meaningfully.

"Maybe if you worked a little harder, some crimes would get solved around here," Thane heard Grady mutter under her breath.

"Grady! Why don't you go inside and get us some coffee for the ride."

"Make sure you give him lots of sugar," Opie said.

Grady took a step in his direction, but Thane reached out and pulled her back onto the path.

"Please, Grady," Thane said in a low voice. Her shoulders came down and without a word she walked down the steep hill and disappeared into the cabin.

Opie walked in to the open barn and cursed appreciatively. "You did that?" He pointed to the bedframe and the scene imprinted into the headboard.

"No, Grady did."

Opie gave a grunt and shrugged as he crouched to pick up one end of a bench as Thane took the other.

It didn't take long to get everything loaded. Thane went to the cab to get out some rope to tie it all down, but Jim blocked his way, his arms crossed.

"You slept with her, didn't you?"

Technically, yes. But not the way he'd wanted to.

Opie took his silence for an answer and swore. "That was fast."

"It's not what you think," Thane said.

Opie snorted. "I never thought you'd be the one to get your head all twisted around. Cal, anytime, any woman, but you?"

"There's a side to her you haven't seen."

"I bet there is, and I bet you saw it all night long."

Thane's eyes narrowed. "Opie, I'm warning you."

"And I'm warning you," he responded. "I know you got a habit of picking up strays and giving them a good home," he said nodding at Beau. Then he cocked his head meaningfully towards the house, towards Grady. "But this bitch doesn't need—"

Without thinking, without waiting to hear what Grady did or didn't need, Thane took his best friend by the grey collar of his uniform and slammed him against the pickup's door. Opie wasn't surprised. The smirk on his face said he was testing Thane, and he had failed the test. Or passed it, depending on the perspective.

Thane watched the smirk fade as he said tightly: "I'd appreciate if you wouldn't talk that way. About my wife."

Opie stared at him for a moment. "Now that you got yourself a princess, you know what that makes you? A real prince."

Thane let him go and took a step back.

"You're in over your head, buddy, now. But it's not too late to get rid of her," Opie said as he pushed himself away from the truck and straightened his jacket with a tight tug.

"Until you prove she set fire to that shed, or find the guy who did it, she's not going anywhere." Thane said.

Opie cursed. "I'm working on it, In fact, by tomorrow, if things go as planned, there won't be a reason for her to stay."

"Are you that close?"

"The question is, how close are the two of you?"

Not as close as his friend thought. Not as close as Thane wanted to be.

"I don't know why I bother," Opie said as he got into his cruiser. "Good luck," he added.

"Hopefully I won't need luck. You've seen what an artist Grady is. I think we've got a real chance of placing in the competition."

"I wasn't talking about the competition," Opie said as he pulled away faster than he needed to go.

Inside the cabin, Grady changed into a tapered blue blouse with just the barest of sleeves Thane had bought her, and her usual jeans. She'd promised to pay him back, but for now it was borrowed—something borrowed, something blue. That was a saying for a wedding, a new beginning. But she felt like something was ending. The siren on Oplin's Crown Royal had signaled it; the real world was intruding again. After today, Thane wouldn't need her any more.

She put a pot of coffee on, but didn't make breakfast. She wasn't hungry. Finally she heard the patrol car spit gravel as it made its way back out to route 9. Only then did she leave the house, with a cup of coffee for Thane, which was by now cold.

"Thanks, just put it in the truck, please," he said in a stiff voice.

She watched him pull the ropes taut that would hold the furniture in place along the winding back roads on the 45-minute trip to the Adirondack Museum.

He was just about finished when he looked up and out towards the road. Grady heard it too, the crunch of tires on gravel.

"What's he come back for now?" she muttered.

"It's not Jim," he said, and he was right as a Buick, wide as a boat, turned around the bend. "It's not anyone to me," he continued.

"You're wrong, Thane," Grady said, and her voice sounded small even to her. "You're about to meet your in-laws."

Grady forced herself to take a step forward as her mother and Richard Hartwell stepped out of their car. Richard was the kind of man who didn't really age. He could have been 50, he could have been 70. He wore a perfectly tailored sport jacket and a perfect tan.

Her mother was only 45, but had done her hair up in a tight twist, and wore a black elegant suit with severe lines to make herself look older and more sophisticated. Grady saw her mother's eyes travel disapprovingly from the dusty gravel road to Thane's old pickup, to Thane himself, to Grady and then to the weathered barn. Suddenly her eyes flew back.

"Grady?! What are you doing here?"

Grady hadn't wanted to be found, but a deep childish hurt rose up in Grady as she realized her mother hadn't been looking for her at all. It grew deeper as her mother took a step towards her.

"I didn't even recognize you. Oh, Grady, you're a mess. You know they can't cut hair up here." She reached out to cup Grady's chin in her ringed hand, but Grady took a step back and bumped into Thane.

"What do you want from me, Mom?"

"From you? We were looking for Duane McMasters. No one at Sterling Construction could tell us a thing. They said he would know what the hold up was on the renovations for the cabin."

"This is Thane, Mom. Thane McMasters. And you weren't planning a renovation. I think the word you're looking for is demolition."

"Grady," Richard Hartwell spoke now. "There was extensive water damage from the pipes leaking."

"That doesn't make sense. You told me you'd take care of everything when Dad died. You said you'd hire someone to winterize it."

He shrugged. "It's tough to get good help up here."

She wondered if he had even tried. "There had to be something salvageable."

"It would have been more trouble than it was worth," he said.

"Not to me! To me it was worth everything. If you had just asked me!"

"Grady, I don't think you would have seen reason, even if we had."

All she saw now was red.

"We'd like to know what's going on here," he went on. The building site is a mess, the shed's been burned."

"Fred Morey didn't tell you?" Grady asked in surprise.

Grady's mother looked at her new husband and then back to Grady. "He said you're petitioning the trust to turn over the funds to you. But Grady, you know that can't happen until you're 25."

"Sandy," Hartwell said in a cautioning tone. "We can discuss that later in private."

"The tenets say 25, or married," Grady reminded them.

Her mother laughed. "Oh, Grady, who are you going to marry?"

"The question you need to be asking is who did I marry."

She thought she heard Hartwell curse under his breath. "Oh, Grady, what have you gone and gotten yourself into now?" he said as he came a step closer. "Thane, would you mind giving us a little privacy so we can talk?"

Grady answered for him. "I'd prefer my husband stay, since this involves him too."

Her mother's eyes went wide. "Him?"

Grady turned to Thane with an apologetic smile. "Welcome to the family."

Sandy Hartwell sighed. "This isn't what you want, Grady," she said.

"No, Mom, this isn't what you want. Why doesn't anyone ask me what I want?"

"Grady," Richard Hartwell said in a sharp voice. "I don't think you realize what you've done. But it shouldn't be too late to undo it."

"I know exactly what I've done."

"Do you? He could sue you for your inheritance."

"The lawyer told me that would be considered separate from marital assets," she said.

Hartwell took a step closer. "He could still sue. You'd eat up your trust in legal fees."

"He would never sue," Grady said, but Hartwell rolled right over her.

"Or demand maintenance. Have you really thought about that Grady, about what that means? Do you want a stranger spending the money your father worked so hard to make, so hard it took a toll on his health?"

She stared back pointedly. "I'm used to someone else spending my father's money."

He didn't flinch. "Maybe it's best if we sell the property Grady, it's no good to anyone in this state," he said casually.

"You are not selling it!" Grady sputtered.

"Richard knows what he's doing, Grady. He knows how to manage money. He knows what's best," her mother said.

"For himself," Grady amended.

Richard Hartwell put a protective or a warning arm around his wife's shoulder. "It's time to go, honey. We'll see if we can track down this Cal Sterling. I think he'll understand our dilemma."

"Don't bother. I already paid him to stop construction."

Hartwell's mouth went down. "We'll talk about this more when you've had a chance to calm down," he said. "In the meantime, let's solve the most pressing problem. You made a mistake, Grady," he continued. "I can understand that. You're hurting. And I think Thane here can understand that too, can't you?"

He didn't expect an answer. He pulled his checkbook and a pen from his inside pocket and used the hood of Thane's Ranger as a desk.

"This is for any inconvenience," he said lightly as if Grady were a kid who had hit a baseball through his window. "You'll get the same amount once the divorce papers are signed and filed. I think you'll see this is the best way. We'd rather not be forced to contest this marriage in court."

Grady's heart stopped as Thane reached out a hand, and glanced down at the figure written in Richard's neat script.

"It's her money," Thane said, passing the check to Grady. "I told her when we got married, I wouldn't take it, and I'm not going to start now."

"So what do you want, then?" Richard Hartwell pressed.

"Nothing you could give me." Thane said tightly.

Grady looked at him. She couldn't have picked a better man for a husband if she'd tried. The only problem was, he hadn't picked her. Given the chance, would he?

"Is it true?" Grady asked Thane once her mother and Richard Hartwell had left. "That the cabin couldn't have been saved? That there was too much water damage?"

Thane sighed. He didn't like Richard Hartwell. He didn't like getting put in the middle.

"It was pretty far gone," he said.

"But it could have been saved?"

He shrugged. "Anything can be saved, I guess, with enough money, even if it's just the shell. But that's all it would have been, just a facade."

She nodded, but he couldn't read her.

"Speaking of money, Grady, I had no idea that I'd be entitled to anything in a divorce. You know I wouldn't take anything from you."

"I know," she said. "I know that," she repeated, as she looked away and her shoulders dropped, but it didn't seem with relief. There was a tension in her. He chalked it up to their meeting with the Hartwells.

He turned from her. "We'd better get going," he said, opening the cab and pushing Beau into the middle and getting in.

As soon as Grady was buckled, Thane put the truck in drive and looked up in time to stop as Dan Hardin tottered across the driveway a foot in front of his hood. Thane cursed. "What is it now, Dan?" he asked bluntly as he glanced at the clock on his dash.

"Nothing for you," Hardin growled as he stuck his head around Grady's side. "I came to wish this little lady some luck." His expression changed. His milky eyes brightened as he handed Grady a box made of smooth cedar. "You'll need it to put all that cash in. Maybe I should have made it bigger."

Grady gasped. "It's beautiful."

"Aw, it's just a box," Dan blustered, but his cheek, his freshly-shaven cheek, Thane noticed, reddened as she kissed it. "Now get out of here," he commanded, stepping away, but not before giving the side of the truck a hard slap with his cane.

"That's what I've been trying to do," Thane muttered. "We're not stopping for any more visitors," he said to Grady. "Even if it means I have to run them down." He didn't know it, but Dan was not going to be the last.

Chapter Eleven

This wasn't the real Adirondacks. Here at the museum in Blue Mountain Lake, the rough cabins stood straight as soldiers, the lawns manicured and unthreatening. Out there in the rest of the park, gravity pulled at the roof ridges, and vines worked their way up and in. Nature was a steady, if slow, wrecking ball. Grady knew that first-hand. Her cabin couldn't have been saved, not its heart anyway. But she would have wanted the chance to at least try.

Grady tied a tag around the post of the bedframe Thane had made. It read 'sold.' It had placed third in the Rustic Furniture competition, and a couple from New York City had already put a down payment on it. Thane had gone with them to the parking lot to see if it would fit in their trailer, or if he'd have to dismantle part of it. Beau for now was using it as temporary shade from the hot sun.

The day had been a success. They'd won, but this felt like another loss to Grady. She'd spent so much time working on the bed, all the while picturing it in Thane's loft. But now it was as good as gone, and Grady would soon be too. He wasn't the kind of man to order her to leave, but she understood his message. "I wouldn't take anything from you," he'd said.

A copy of the bill of sale lay on the frame and she picked it up. She looked at the price, still not sure she'd heard right. It was astronomical. Then she noticed the way Thane had listed the seller: as Thane and Grady McMasters. There was little room, and he did it to save space, she told herself, but still her heart jumped.

Beau did too at the same time and began to bark. To grab his collar with both hands, she had to let the bill of sale go and it fluttered into the path of an older couple as they approached.

The woman rubbed Beau energetically behind the ears, while the man with her bent down and picked up the piece of paper. He glanced at it as he straightened, showed it to the woman next to him and then gave Grady a sharp glance. His height made her feel small. He looked down to read her name slowly off the form. "Is that you?"

"Yes," she said, as she reached out to take it from him.

"And Thane McMasters," he said. "Would that be your husband?"

"Well, um, yes," Grady faltered.

He brought the full brunt of his brown eyes on her, as he ran his hand through his short, greying brown hair in a gesture that seemed familiar.

"If you could tell him I'd like to talk to him, I'd appreciate it."

"Could I get your name?" Grady asked, trying to remain polite.

"Well," he said, looking off in the distance to Blue Mountain as if searching the summit for something. "I guess you can call me Dad."

When Thane returned to the display area, he was already expecting the worst. He'd seen the Voyager travel trailer in the parking lot with Florida plates, so it didn't surprise him to see his parents. Even from a distance, he saw the rigidity in his father's bowed shoulders. As he got closer, he could see his mother biting her lip like she always did when something worried her.

Beau was the first one to sense him approach, and he lunged towards Thane, almost taking Grady off her feet who was holding him by his collar.

She turned to him with wide eyes. "Thane! These are your parents," she said.

"I know, Grady, I recognize them." He hugged his mother, and she seemed brittle in his arms. His father returned his handshake, and his grip was hard. Thane took hold of Beau's collar, so he wouldn't keep Grady off balance.

She stumbled over her words instead. "I was just telling them that it wasn't what it looked like."

"So you're not married, then?" Thane's father crossed his arms.

"No, we are ... it's just ... it's hard to explain," she said.

"We would have come back earlier had we known. I could have helped you with the plans," his mother said and her olive eyes radiated hurt.

Grady stumbled on. "It happened so fast. There was nothing to plan. It was just us and the justice of the peace." Grady looked from one to the other and began to talk faster as if she could erase their expressions of growing hurt and confusion. "I was having trouble with my family. I was in a situation. But it's all going to be taken care of in a week so we don't need to stay married."

Thane's mother gasped. His father swore. "Jeezum crow, son. You like a girl enough to get her into trouble, you damn well better like her enough to stay married."

"No! It's not what you think. I'm not having his baby."

His mother reached out a hand and touched Grady's cheek. "Oh, Honey, please don't do anything foolish. How far along are you? This is a surprise, but it's a good surprise, isn't it, Bob?"

"She's not pregnant!" Thane lowered his voice as he continued. "She never was pregnant. Look, I can explain everything, but I'd rather not do it here. Why don't you come back to our … I mean my place this evening. You can come for dinner."

"We're pretty tired," Bob McMasters said by way of turning down the invitation. "We stopped in North Carolina last night, then drove straight here because we knew how important it was to you." There was reproach in his voice. "We're heading to our campsite now to get some rest."

"But Bob," his mother protested.

"Marilyn, we're going."

"We'll be there," his mother said.

"Maybe," his father interjected.

"Definitely," his mother rejoined and then they were gone.

Thane turned to Grady. She was focused on far away. He knew that look. She wanted to be gone. Right now he felt like disappearing himself.

Back at his house, Thane watched Grady dish out slices of pizza for him and his parents, and one for herself.

"They were out of toppings," she said as she sat down. Thane could tell she meant it to be apologetic, and his mother nodded sympathetically. His father heard a complaint.

"Damn lucky to have a pizza parlor here at all. When I was growing up, we got our pizza from the gas station. Never had a supermarket, either. Had to drive 30 miles if we wanted something other than milk and eggs." He looked hard at Grady. "You're not from around here are you?"

"My Dad was from here, I grew up on Long Island."

"What's the last name again?" he said to Thane.

"Henderson."

He thought for a moment. "There were Hendersons over at Pilot Point."

Grady nodded.

"Your father was William?"

"You knew him?"

"Knew of him, he was a bit younger than me. Good hunter. He and Moose bagged the biggest buck in the park some years back, I heard. If they'd done it during hunting season, they probably would have held some kind of record," he said disapprovingly.

"Not many people stick it out here for the long haul," his father kept going, and Thane heard the insinuation that Grady's people weren't tough enough to handle it. He glanced at Grady, she hadn't taken a bite of her pizza, but she'd looked like she'd swallowed something that had gone bad.

Thane's mother cleared her throat. "Winters can be so long," she agreed. "That's why we go to Florida, isn't it Bob?"

"How'd you two meet anyway?" Thane's father asked.

"Bob!" his wife said to him.

"I'm just making conversation."

"Well it sounds like an interrogation," she said.

It was. Grady sat with her back to the kitchen. They had pushed the table towards the living room to make space and the kitchen light hung over her, making shadows of her eyes. Thane had had hours to prepare for this conversation, but still hadn't come up with a good way to start it. He hesitated, and Grady filled the vacuum.

"Thane was, um, doing some work on my Dad's cabin."

"And when was this?" Bob McMasters asked.

"About three weeks ago," Grady said softly.

"You marry a girl after only knowing her three weeks?"

"No, he married me the day after he met me," Grady answered.

His father cursed, which wasn't like him at all. He was upset. So was Thane.

"Dad, please." Thane pushed his plate away. He'd lost his appetite. "I'll ask you not to use that word around her."

"Word?! I don't understand a word this girl is saying."

"They were tearing the cabin down and I tried to stop them," Grady said haltingly. "Jack Hanson would have run me over with his bulldozer if Thane hadn't pushed me out of the way, and then it gets a little fuzzy. Trooper Oplin showed up and he got hit accidentally."

"With the dozer? Is Opie all right?"

"No, with my hand. I'm not sure how. Everything happened so fast and all at once and I have trouble remembering it, and then the out shed on the property happened to catch fire."

"Happened to?"

"Well, Oplin thinks I did it, but how could I have?"

Thane's father looked back and forth between the two of them. "I don't understand why she isn't in jail for assaulting an officer of the law."

"Judge Mullens remanded her to my care because they didn't have the manpower to take her down to the Warren County Jail," Thane said.

For a moment there was silence, as Grady stared at her untouched pizza, and his parents stared at Grady. Thane's mother had put her hand over her mouth. His father had nothing to silence him. "I still don't understand why you're married? Did the judge hold a shotgun to your head, son?"

"Dad!" Thane said in a warning voice.

Grady laid a hand lightly on Thane's arm. "It's okay, Thane. They have a right to know." Then she turned back to his father.

"I wanted to put a lien on the cabin to stop any construction on it,

Thane agreed to marry me if I didn't do it."

"But I don't understand,"

"It would have put Cal out of business, my stepfather was basically his only client."

"But why'd you have to go and marry our boy, why is it so important for you to be somebody's wife?"

"I had to get access to the trust my father left for me, to get the cabin, or what's left of it out of my stepfather's control ... and to make bail. The rules of the trust say I couldn't access it until I was 25...or married."

"How old are you now?"

"23."

"So you married him for money."

Grady sighed. "For my money. There's a difference."

"Maybe so, but that still doesn't make it right. Marriage isn't some joke."

"I know that," Grady said. Her mouth twitched, and instead of saying anything she got up, dumped her pizza into the garbage, and set her plate in the sink.

"Would anyone like tea? Coffee?" she asked in a normal voice. Or it would have sounded normal to anyone else, but Thane knew her. It was a thin sheet of ice, and he was afraid they'd all go crashing through it.

"I don't understand. If she can make bail, why the hell isn't she gone already?"

"Dad, ease up. There's a 30-day waiting period for the trust to release funds," Thane said.

"And when is that up?"

"In a week."

Grady began pulling out mugs from a cabinet.

"So in seven days you can start the divorce."

"That was the plan." Thane said softly.

"Was?!" His father looked at him with wide eyes. "I hope you mean 'is!' I hope that's soon enough, before she makes herself even more at home."

A cup rattled hard against a saucer, but otherwise Grady gave no indication she had heard. Thane was trying hard to see this all through his father's eyes. It was a difficult story to tell and a difficult one to hear. Hell, Thane had lived through it and still couldn't believe it. It was like retelling a car accident, it was hard to reconstruct that piece of the past, let alone get his parents to understand how he could imagine Grady in his future.

His father continued. "There are other ways to help a friend without letting a girl like this drag you down."

"That's it," Thane said quietly. "You need to go."

Grady turned to look at Thane, shaking her head, her eyes wide. At the same time his father was nodding as if in approval.

"No," she said quietly.

"I wasn't talking to you, Grady," Thane said in a softer voice.

"I know," she said in almost a whisper. "Please don't do this."

But he'd made up his mind. He pushed his chair back hard, opened the door and for a second time asked his father to leave.

It took a long moment for his father to get up, for the realization to come into his eyes and then the disappointment.

"I'm sorry, honey, he'll come around," his mother said as she got up and passed Grady.

"No he won't," Thane said. "He won't be coming around here, not until he apologizes."

"I thought I raised you to know better, son."

Thane did know better. All of a sudden, the knowledge that had been creeping up on him about Grady was crystal clear.

"There's nothing wrong with the way you raised me, Dad. But I find something wrong with the way you're talking about my wife."

Thane held the screen door open for his parents. His father walked out, his back rigid, his mouth shut in a grim line. His mother squeezed his hand as she left, and Thane let the door close. There was something final about it. They were on one side, he was on the other. On Grady's side. Something had ended, and in a perfect world something new could begin, if Grady would only let it. He turned to her, but she had her back to him at the kitchen sink. A moth had slipped through the open door and was flinging itself uselessly at the bulb above the sink. Thane didn't know how to start.

The house was so quiet now that Thane's parents had left. Beau was asleep. The heat seemed to slow the rhythm of the crickets. The window above the sink was open as far as it would go, but there was no breeze to catch and pull inside.

Grady had lost her own father and now she'd made Thane push his away. His father had been right, not that she was a spoiled princess, but that she was dragging him down.

There were few dishes to clean up, but she took her time washing them.

Thane came to the sink and stood beside her, his hip resting against the countertop. "It's not your fault," he said quietly.

She nodded. He would think she was agreeing with him, but she was saying yes, it was her fault. All of this had been her fault. She'd gone crazy, had stood in front of a bulldozer, had assaulted an officer of the law and had gotten Thane into her mess. She had cost him his friends, now it was his family.

He put a hand on her arm. "Grady," he said. "Look at me."

She did for just the briefest moment. She tried to memorize those serious brown eyes and tried not to think about how much she was going to miss them. In that second, she also saw that he knew she was going to run. She didn't want him to stop her, but something inside her ached when he didn't say anything to try to change her mind. He wouldn't be able to, but if he'd tried, she would have known she had meant something to him.

She looked down at the plates in the sink. The pressure on her arm increased ever so slightly, but she didn't look up again. And after awhile, without saying another word, Thane let her go.

Chapter Twelve

Thane lay on the couch staring into the darkness of the cathedral ceiling. High above him, the tongue and groove pine was holding in the heat, pushing it down on him. His father's words kept coming back to him. He had referred to Grady as a 'girl like this.'

Thane had been looking for a long time for a girl like this. And now he'd found her. He'd been fighting it, because of the way they'd met. She'd been pushed into his life by the judge, by circumstance. And he didn't want to let her go.

Could it be that easy? He laughed quietly to himself. Life with Grady Henderson would certainly not be easy. But it could be rewarding. He'd seen that already in the way they worked together. He wanted to do more with her than work.

But he wouldn't get the chance if he let her go and he knew she was about to run.

What could he say to get her to stay? Heat lightning erased the darkness for a brief flickering instant and Thane waited for the thunder. It didn't come. It was an empty threat with nothing behind it. Empty words were not going to make Grady stay.

Beside him on the floor, Beau began to snore softly. And a few minutes later, he heard the bed upstairs creak as Grady got out of it. Did she think it was him snoring? His quick smile wilted in the heat. If he hadn't been on watch, he wouldn't have heard her light step on the stairs, and the long pause between each tread. She was giving him more time to come up with the right things to say, but it didn't matter. Nothing was coming to him.

When she got to the bottom of the staircase, she had to pass close by the couch. It was so dark, he could only make out her form, and how she stood over him for a long time. Would she say something? No, she was turning. But she wouldn't leave, because in one movement, he swung himself up to a sitting position, reached out and grabbed for her in the dark. He caught a fistful of her soft cotton shirt and pulled her down next to him. She didn't cry out in surprise, probably because she'd been so intent on being quiet. That's how stubborn she was. But he heard the sharp intake of her breath.

"Where are you going, Grady?"

She tried to twist away, but he wouldn't let her go. "To get some water."

He believed her. "To take where?" he asked.

He relaxed his grip on her shirt and moved his hand lower along her leg to confirm his suspicions.

"You're wearing jeans, Grady." She was dressed for running away. He left his hand on her thigh, just above her knee to keep her there.

"Where are you going to go?" he pressed.

In the darkness he could feel her shrug.

"How are you going to get there?"

Another shrug.

"You promised me you'd stay." His voice came out louder, angrier than he'd intended. But he was angry!

"I kept my promise. You asked me to stay until the competition was over."

Thane blew out a breath. "What about the orders we got? Those people are expecting to get what they saw today. I can't do that without you. I need you Grady."

"Need," she echoed him quietly. "You're better off without me. I cost you your friends. And now your family. No one wants me here," she said. And she was right for the most part. His friends didn't like her, his parents didn't trust her. But he wasn't thinking of them.

"What about me, Grady?"

"What about you?" she asked softly, and he thought he heard her voice catch, like she was afraid to know the answer.

"I want you. Here."

"You can't possibly. I've caused you so much trouble."

Thane sighed. "What can I say to make you believe me?"

"Nothing."

She was right, nothing he'd say would change her mind.

The heat lightning illuminated the inside of the cabin like a sudden x-ray, and he caught a glimpse of her profile as she looked down at her hands and how she was turning the ring around and around on her finger. Her wedding ring. Then the light was gone again, and she disappeared. He didn't want her to be gone.

"Grady," he said into the darkness.

By the sound of her voice, he knew she'd turned to him. "What?"

He found her in the darkness and put a hand on either side of her face and drew her near.

"What were you going to say?" she asked.

"Nothing," he said simply. And then he touched his lips softly to the corner of her mouth. That was his best aim in the dark. Not bad for a start, but he wanted more. He pulled away slightly to try again.

"Did you just kiss me?" she asked quietly, her voice lilting up at the end in surprise.

"Yes."

"Did you mean to?"

"Yes, Grady, I meant to."

He brought his forehead to hers and sighed. Then he kissed her temple, down the side of her cheek. She didn't move. He found the corner of her mouth again this time with his thumb and using it as a guide found her lips with his. He kissed her harder, so she knew it wasn't a mistake. His hand slipped to the back of her neck, his thumb now at the side of her throat.

He paused for a moment, his mouth still on hers, his fingers tangled in her hair at the nape of her neck. She was completely still, like a caught bird, all heartbeat and throbbing pulse.

He went hollow inside. What if she didn't feel the same? He'd thought ... actually he hadn't been doing too much thinking. He'd assumed the attraction he'd felt had been mutual. Had he mistaken her gratitude for something else?

He pulled back, but she moved then, suddenly, her hands at his shirt, her lips following his, so he couldn't break the contact. And he smiled. He gave a soft laugh of relief, and she pulled away, Lightning lit her eyes as she looked up at him. They were wide pools he could drown in. His arms went around her to keep her even closer.

He thought of the first time he'd held her, the day they'd met, when he'd pushed her out of the way of the dozer. He'd been falling for her ever since, for her stubbornness and passion. He pulled her up from the couch and kissed her again and she returned the kiss with a naturalness and an honesty that shouldn't have surprised him. He took her hand, and he could feel the ring on her finger. They were married in name only. He was going to change that.

His mouth never left hers as he guided her up the stairs backwards to the loft, not stopping until they stumbled against the bed. Very gently he laid her down and as he stood over her, lightning sparked again, crackling along the edges of the heat, illuminating her long form, the way she looked at him with wide eyes, the way she waited for him. And then in the darkness that followed he found his way along her body with his hands and then with his mouth. And as the heat continued to press against them in the still black night, he made Grady Henderson his wife.

Grady awoke to find Thane, head propped on his hand, watching her.

In the grainy light she felt suddenly self-conscious about the things they'd done in the cover of night. "Good morning," she mumbled.

A slow smile spread on his full lips. "It will be," he said as he rolled her onto her back and covered her with his body, kissing the corner of her mouth. The shyness she felt evaporated suddenly, replaced by other feelings, other needs.

"Was it something I said?" she laughed. He pulled his head back to look at her and his eyes were serious.

"It's everything you do. The way you walk. Those eyes, this neck." He kissed each part as he named them.

The room started to take form around them, but she didn't mind the day returning. As he moved against her, she became all feeling and sensation, so aware of him, of the world, of the way the birds were waking, the way the waves broke softly against the bulkhead below the cabin. Belong, belong, they seemed to whisper. Belong.

Thane had saved her life, and she'd been indebted to him from that day on, and she had paid the debt with her heart. Last night he had taken the rest of her, by giving her everything.

She belonged to Thane now, in more than name. He took her hands in his, pushing them back against the sheets. She felt the ring on his left hand, felt the way her own ring pinched as he clasped her hand harder now as he made her his again, trapping her there beneath him, trapping her hands in his. She'd never felt more free.

Chapter Thirteen

Thane couldn't remember the last time he'd slept in. Not that he and Grady had done much sleeping. She hadn't had much experience, he could tell, even without asking. She had never let someone this close. And she was rewarding Thane with everything she'd missed out on.

All the things that had gotten her into trouble, her fearlessness, her passion, her natural unfiltered response left him satisfied and still wanting more from her. His hands had tangled themselves in her short hair when the phone rang. He ignored it and pulled her in for another kiss. Finally the answering machine kicked in. He felt Grady go rigid against him, as a female voice sounded his name.

They both recognized it, they both heard the panic in it. Grady pulled her head back and looked at him as Shauna's voice came over the answering machine.

"Thane? Grady? If you're there, please pick up. Jim didn't come home last night. I thought he'd picked up another shift, but I just called the station, he wasn't due in. Are you there? His backpack is gone, his hiking stuff. Did he tell you what he was up to? Thane, I need you."

Thane was up out of bed, scrambling into the pair of jeans he picked up from the floor. Grady was dressing just as quickly.

She was close behind him as he lunged down the stairs and caught the phone. He had nothing to offer Shauna. He had no idea where Jim was going, what he might have been planning. All he could do was promise Shauna he'd get to the municipal center where she told him they were setting up search teams.

"Stay here," he said to Grady after he'd hung up, but the spell of last night when she would do anything he demanded was broken.

She followed him out to the Ranger.

"He's at Hoffman's mine," Grady said as soon as she and Thane had gotten into the pickup, Beau whining nervously between them. Thane didn't respond. He didn't say a word, even when they reached the municipal center.

Uniformed men were moving up and down the corridors. In a conference room off the hallway a group of state troopers were leaning over a large map on a small table. Thane hesitated at the doorway, but Grady stepped inside

"He's at Hoffman's mine," she said.

The trooper with the most stripes on his uniform took her in for a moment, then his eyes flitted to his comrades. "Who the hell is this?"

Comments floated out towards the hallway. 'Princess.' 'Broke his nose.'

"Haven't you caused enough trouble?" the trooper asked as he turned his back on her.

Thane pulled Grady out of the conference room.

"But he's there! In the garnet mine, I know it," she said in a hushed voice.

Thane rubbed his forehead. Did she mean Jim, or the guy she'd imagined?

He put a hand out and stopped a trooper he recognized from Jim's troop.

"I'd like to help look for him. He's my friend."

The trooper brushed him off. "Leave it to the professionals, buddy. Looks like we got one guy who needs rescuing, we don't need any more."

Grady didn't say anything. She didn't have to. Her eyes were pleading. Thane looked at her a long moment and then took her by the elbow.

"Let's go," he said.

Back in the truck he stopped at the intersection and put his blinker on to make the left onto Route 9.

"No!" Grady said. "Take the dump road. Go around to the trail head. It's a rougher hike in, but shorter."

He hesitated for a minute then decided she was right.

He could have told her this wasn't her fault. Her rigid shoulders told him she wouldn't believe him. But it was true.

When Jim had helped him load the furniture yesterday, he'd asked when Thane would be back. If it weren't for Grady, maybe Jim would have asked Thane to go with him to the mine, if that's really where he'd been headed.

But this wasn't Grady's fault. It was Thane's.

Grady and Thane hadn't been prepared for a hike. They had no water with them, no backpack, no emergency blanket, or whistle. Thane had brought his cellphone with him, but with no reception at the brink of the Hoffman pit mine, that was useless too. Out of breath, Grady leaned over, put her hands on her knees and scanned the rocky crevices. Beau dropped next to her, too exhausted to bark. This had always been such a magical place, but the sky was mean, the clouds heavy and without the sun the garnet couldn't sparkle. It had lost its magic.

She started to believe that maybe she'd been wrong, Jim hadn't come here, when Thane touched her arm. "I see him!" he said.

Grady followed his outstretched hand, and there at the base of the far rough wall of rock, she saw Jim Oplin, or rather saw the soles of his boots, one splayed at an unnatural angle.

"Stay here." Thane was already moving towards the sharp slope.

She grabbed his arm. "No! Let me go. You'll be that much quicker to get help, to get back into cell range, if. . ." she couldn't complete the sentence. "You told me you don't know CPR. My Dad made sure I was trained in first aid. It makes sense, Thane, please."

"If this guy ... if someone is down there with him—"

"Do you see anyone?"

"No, but—"

"Beau will be with me."

"I told you, he's no hero, Grady."

"If someone's down there, they won't know that. Please, Thane, we may not have much time."

He hesitated for a moment, then put a hand briefly to her cheek.

"Go," he said with clenched teeth.

It didn't take Grady long at all to make the descent; she stumbled over an outcropping of rock and went tumbling down. But it took her longer than she'd thought to reach Jim because the floor of the pit was overgrown with roots and brush that hid treacherous depressions. Beau, making a noise between a whimper and a snarl, caught up with her as she reached Jim and kneeled by his side.

She held her breath while she bent over him and put two shaking fingers to the base of his neck. It took her a while to find a pulse. It was weak, but it was there.

She rocked back on her heels and put a hand on Beau's back in relief. It was only then that she noticed the way his hair stood up. She turned her head to see what he was looking at.

She had passed within a few feet of the figure and had never even noticed him crouched down on his haunches. Probably because he was so filthy, it was hard to tell him apart from the dead brown leaves and orange pine needles that carpeted the floor of the mine. Grady froze for a moment staring at the man, who stared back at her with wide eyes.

The way Jim lay spoke for a fall. If this person meant further harm, he would have done it. He would have already taken the gun from Jim's belt, wouldn't he have? Unless he hadn't seen it.

Very slowly Grady reached for Jim's holster, undid the latch and pulled the Glock towards her and took the safety off. Jim's eyelids fluttered. It's okay, she wanted to say, but she wasn't sure if it was. "Do you know who I am?" she asked him instead.

Jim stared at her and then his eyes narrowed. He responded in what was barely a whisper with two words, neither of which were her name, but she didn't mind the insult. His pulse beat stronger against her finger, even as he went slack and unconscious.

"It's going to be okay," Grady said to his unconscious form. The figure across from her began to rock back and forth and the movement caught her eye. She looked up. "It's going to be okay," she said, even as she held the gun in his direction. Or tried. It wavered in her shaking hand. She wouldn't have been able to hit him even at this close range.

Thunder grumbled along the ridge of the mine and Beau whimpered. Grady scanned the area. About ten feet away but hard to spot was a dirty brown tarp strung on a line between two young saplings. She stood up slowly on shaking legs, walking backwards so she could watch Jim, and the filthy stranger. One hand still on the gun, it took her a while to rip the tarp off the line and then she came back and covered Jim as the rain started to come in fat drops. A clap of thunder sent Beau cowering under the tarp, and Grady sank down next to it. There was another piece of plastic at the makeshift campsite, but Grady didn't trust her legs to go and get it.

It was going to be okay. She put her hand under the tarp, felt again for Jim's pulse. It thudded quietly against her fingers as the rain began to beat down hard and steady. It was going to be okay. His sons wouldn't have to grow up with a piece of themselves missing.

Grady had been too angry to cry when she'd lost her own father. The tears wouldn't come at his funeral, but they ran down Grady's cheeks now as if the rain was helping them remember how to fall. All the anger and the pain and the loss shook her like the thunder that echoed again against the rough walls of the pit mine. She kept the Glock pointed in the general direction of the figure whose dirty wiry hair was turning even darker in the rain, but as inconspicuously as she could she put the safety back on.

"It's going to be okay," she said between sobs. And the figure with wide eyes looked back at her like she was crazy.

The storm had almost spent itself. Grady didn't feel cold. Not even as the helicopter hovered low overhead as Jim was loaded carefully onto a stretcher and hauled up into its belly. The hunched and dirty figure who had watched everything happen, had been led away. Someone had taken the gun from Grady's hand. There was a blanket around her wet shoulders, but she wasn't sure how it had gotten there. A medic was sticking a thermometer into her ear.

Thane stood in front of her, arms crossed. All she wanted to do was go home, but the trooper next to him had some questions for her.

"You put the tarp over Jim?"

She nodded.

"Was it your idea to put the dog in there with him? Probably saved him from hypothermia, that and the fact it was so damn warm last night."

"No, it was Beau's idea."

"That kook?"

"No, Beau's the dog."

"The dog's a hero," he said.

Grady looked up and tried to smile at Thane.

Rain dripped from the rim of the trooper's hat. "Did he say anything?"

"He just sat there watching, I don't think he meant to do any harm."

"Not the crazy bastard. I meant Jim."

She nodded as someone handed her a cup of strong coffee.

"Well, what did he say?"

"Fuck you," she murmured as she took a drink of the strong coffee.

"You really are a piece of work. This is an investigation, damn it."

"No! That's what Jim said to me! I took his gun from his holster and he opened his eyes."

Another few troopers had come around. "Instinct," she heard one mutter.

"I called his name, but he wasn't focusing," she went on. "I asked him if he knew who I was and that's when he said that."

Laughter seemed to spread across the mine where other uniformed men were bending over the rough ground looking for evidence.

"He knew you all right, princess!" the first trooper said, giving her a not-so-gentle pat on the shoulder that made her spill the coffee onto her jeans. The contrast of the hot liquid seemed to remind her suddenly that she was cold. She started to shiver.

The medic was undoing a blood pressure sleeve from her arm. "We should probably admit you just in case."

"I just want to go home," she said.

The trooper stood watching with his arms crossed. "Where's that? Long Island? Four-hour trip is not a good idea."

"No. I meant ..." She looked at Thane.

"She's coming home with me," he said as he stepped forward and pulled her up. "My truck's parked at the header. My house is just around the other side of Garnet Lake."

"We'll get you guys out of here on a four-wheeler."

Mike Mullens arrived as they were leaving. He put a hand on her shoulder. "You all right, Grady?"

She forced a nod. "That guy, whatever he did, whatever happened, he didn't mean it."

"You know what that's like, huh?" he said without malice.

Then he turned to Thane. "Take care of her."

"I plan to," Thane said.

Grady couldn't stop shaking, not in the truck with the heater on full blast and Beau's wet fur plastered to her jeans. A hot shower at Thane's cabin didn't help either. She didn't stop shivering until Thane laid her down in his bed in the loft and crawled under the covers with her. He didn't tell her things would be okay. He didn't say anything at all. She took the warmth from him. She had nothing to give in return, but he didn't seem to mind as he kissed away the cold and finally her thoughts, until there was only room for him.

Then he was leaving, tucking the blankets around her and she tried to pull him back to her, but she couldn't hold him. The last thing she heard before she fell asleep were his steps on the loft stairs.

Thane didn't care if visiting hours were over, he drove down to Albany Med and walked past the reception area and the nurse's station. But he couldn't get past the locked doors at ICU. He paced the hallway, until Shauna came out. She wasn't in any state to talk, but she nodded. That was a good sign. She went into his arms and it was a while before she could give him an update. One of the ledges at the mine had given way under his weight and had taken Jim down with it.

He had more than a few broken ribs, one of which had punctured his lung. His right knee was so messed up he may never walk right again. Add to that a sprained wrist and a concussion and multiple lacerations especially on his hands from when he had tried to keep himself from falling. None of those things would have killed him, but the hypothermia came close.

"You can go home, Thane," Shauna said. "My in-laws are here, I'll be okay."

Thane hadn't been there for his friend when it had counted, he could never make up for that, but the least he could do was stick around now.

There wasn't much he could do, except nod off during the night in a metal chair. But at least he was there when they wheeled Jim out of ICU in the morning and transferred him to a room in the next wing. He was there when Jim's eyes fluttered open for a moment. He was there to see what looked like pain, resignation and fear. Jim was a man who hated weakness ... in himself. He thought he could do anything, and it had caused him to take risks before, but now he'd been proven wrong, and Thane didn't know how his friend was going to learn to live with that. Thane was trying to learn to live with his own regrets. He thought about Grady. She wasn't a regret, could never be, but what had he given up to get her?

Chapter Fourteen

Three mornings later, Thane woke Grady. "We've got to go," he said.

"Go where?"

"Didn't Shauna tell you?"

"What?"

"The higher-ups want a picture of you and Jim to put a story in the paper."

"Why me?"

"Because you saved his life."

She may have been instrumental in finding him, but she'd also egged him on. It was her fault he'd gone to the mine in the first place.

"But I can't imagine Jim would want me in the same room with him let alone in a picture. I don't think this is a good idea," she said.

"Yeah, but the idea's coming from pretty high up. Jim's getting a commendation, and a promotion. A lot of good it does him! The guy he found in the woods is a distant relative of the Governor. He went off his medication five years ago and his family had been searching for him ever since. It's out of our hands, Grady, come on, get dressed, let's just get it over with."

Thane went downstairs and she could hear him making coffee. She thought about putting on her only dress, but it didn't seem appropriate. She wore her blue blouse instead and her jeans. By the time she was ready, he was already in the truck waiting for her. She hadn't had breakfast which was fine, she wasn't hungry.

When she opened the passenger door, Beau brushed past her and in. At first she laughed at the way he sat there with his hind legs on the seat like a human. But after a few moments of trying to coax him out, she was no longer laughing.

"I think he's scared to be left alone," she said.

"We'll bring him with us. I can take him for a walk in the parking lot while you're in the hospital."

"You're going to leave me alone with Jim?" she asked as she got in and buckled.

Thane sighed as he pulled out. "Grady, he's not going to do anything to you, he can't even breathe on his own, for God's sake."

Grady hated hospitals. All the stainless steel and white starched uniforms couldn't take the edge off of human suffering. Outside Jim's room, she met Shauna who was signing some papers on a clipboard. Shauna gave her a quick hug and held the door open for her, but didn't go in with her. As it closed behind her, Grady looked at Jim. If he heard her come in, he didn't show it. He stared up at the ceiling.

She cleared her throat. "This wasn't my idea," she said, but he still didn't turn his head, and she wondered if he could. He seemed to have tubes coming out of him in so many places, his nostrils, his mouth, the crook of his arm, that he seemed like a robot. But he knew she was there, she was sure, because very slowly he began to move the fingers of his left hand until all that remained was the middle one. It must have cost him a lot of energy and pain. Instead of the usual sudden rush of anger, Grady just felt sorry for him.

She stood there praying for the photographer to come until Jim made some unintelligible sound and she came closer, leaning in to hear him, but he was silent again.

"I'm sorry," Grady said.

She could barely understand his response. "You should be." The rest of what he said, she wished she couldn't understand, because it was nasty and for the most part untrue.

That sudden flare of anger that had been missing before, came back with extra heat. She was furious with him, not so much for insulting her, but for the risks he had taken. She leaned in close to him. "You thick-headed, stubborn idiot," she began. "What were you thinking going to that mine alone? Any Boy Scout would know better. You want to kill yourself, go ahead, but did you ever think about what you were doing to your wife? To your sons?" Did he narrow his eyes in dislike, or was that a wince? "I saved your life, you ungrateful bastard," she continued. The tension and fear and worry of the last days were coming out now; she was so upset she was almost shaking. "I know what's it's like to lose a father. I saved your boys that pain. The least you could do is say thank you."

His eyes narrowed even further. He didn't say thank you. Instead, managing somehow to get a fistful of her short hair, he banged her head twice against the bedrail, hard.

"Let me go," Grady seethed, and he did, so suddenly she lost her balance. She reached out instinctively, grabbing a fistful of white hospital sheet, but it couldn't keep her from falling. She got tangled in a line of clear plastic tubing as she went down and the room went loud with beeping monitors. By the time she was standing again, the room was filling, orders were being given to reinsert tubes, and Grady was being pushed from the room. And Shauna was pushing her way in.

Grady went over to the nurse's station and grabbed a few rough tissues and held them to her head.

Jim Oplin was Grady's best friend's husband. He was Grady's husband's best friend and that along with the fact he'd almost died couldn't keep him from hating Grady. Nothing, it seemed, had changed.

Grady looked up as Shauna emerged from the room and came at her fast. She didn't even put her hands up. She deserved everything she'd get. But she realized Shauna wasn't hitting her. Shauna was hugging her.

"He's breathing on his own," Shauna said "He's got the fight back in him. I can see it in his eyes. Thank you," she said softly. She gave Grady another squeeze before letting her go and looking pointedly at her forehead. "But Grady do me a favor, and don't come back here, okay?" She turned to go back into Jim's room and looked back over her shoulder. "And don't let that photographer in here."

Grady watched her go. Just how was she going to manage that?

When the man showed up with a bulky camera hanging from his neck, Grady blocked the door to Jim's room. "There's a medical emergency, right now," she told him.

"What about the girl that was involved?" the photographer said.

"That would be me," Grady said, showing him her forehead.

"I came to take a picture of a hero, and I'm not leaving until I get one," he said.

They stood there awkwardly for a moment. Grady thought of Thane and Beau in the parking lot and how she was going to explain her bump. Suddenly she had an idea.

"You want a hero, I've got one." She led the photographer out to the parking lot.

"Beau saved Jim from dying of hypothermia," she said.

When she reached Thane, the photographer approached him.

"So, you're the guy who saved the trooper's life?"

"No," Grady said. "Beau's the dog."

"You've got to be kidding me," he said, even as he was adjusting his camera for the light and instructing Thane on how he wanted Beau posed. It didn't take long and he was gone, still shaking his head.

Grady had kept her face turned away, but now she couldn't avoid Thane any longer. He put a hand under her chin and lifted it towards him.

"What happened?" he asked.

"I fell," she said without meeting his eyes. After a moment he let her go.

All the way up the Northway she thought about how she hadn't exactly lied to her husband. She had fallen, but she'd left a lot of the story out. A marriage needed open communication to work, but there were some things he really didn't need to know.

Chapter Fifteen

Four days later, Grady's trust came through without her even noticing it. She'd been so wrapped up in Jim's recovery and filling orders, working away in the barn, and talking to Shauna in the evenings. During the day she hardly saw Thane. He was either visiting Jim at the rehab facility he'd been moved to, or he was helping Shauna move furniture around to make the Oplin house more accessible when Jim finally came home. In what spare time was left, he was down in Glens Falls picking up supplies and trying to fill the orders he'd picked up at the Rustic Furniture Fair.

Thane was usually gone before Grady even awoke in the mornings, and he would crawl into bed past midnight. In the loft, he and Grady were perfect and whole, no barriers between them as they found each other in the dark, but during the day, Grady couldn't hang on to that closeness.

She was alone in the barn etching a forest scene into the top of a birch nightstand Thane had assembled the night before, when a pickup pulled up and Thane's parents got out. Marilyn McMasters greeted Grady, complimented her on her work and said she was going to take a walk down to the lake. Beau followed her and then Grady was alone with Thane's father.

"I'm sorry this all happened the way it did," he said. "The way you got involved with my son. We waited a long time for Thane, we're a little older, we see things from a different perspective. We want the best for him, not someone who's going to use him."

"I wouldn't do anything to hurt him."

"Why would I believe that?"

"Because I love him."

"How can you love him, you don't even know him."

"But, I do! It's accidental the way things happened. But I couldn't have found a better man if I'd tried. He saved my life—in more ways than one."

"And I don't want you to ruin his, that's all." He paused for a moment. "I guess it doesn't matter how it started. Matters more how it ends, don't you think?"

Grady didn't ever want it to end. But she didn't say anything more. Was he suggesting she leave? It wasn't up to him, though, was it? It was up to Thane. What did he want?

"I hope we understand each other," Thane's father said and Grady didn't respond as she watched him get back into his truck. Thane's mother stepped into the barn then and her face was serious as she looked from her husband's stony profile to Grady's face.

"I'm sorry if you don't think I'm right for Thane," Grady said quietly.

"Is that what the old badger said? Grady, I know from experience the right one for us, isn't always the right one for everyone else. Don't worry about trying to please anyone but your husband. I know you love him."

"Is it that obvious?"

Marilyn McMasters tilted her head and gave Grady a sympathetic smile. She rolled her eyes as her husband tapped on the horn, then she gave Grady a quick hug and was gone. Marilyn McMasters knew Grady loved Thane. But did Thane love Grady?

When Thane came pulling up to the barn a few minutes later, Grady was still standing there thinking about his father's words.

He got out and came around. "I saw my Dad's truck pull out onto Route 9. Did he come to say he was sorry?"

Did he? Grady thought back through the conversation. He'd said he was sorry Grady had gotten involved with his son. That was a long long way from an apology,

Thane put a hand on her shoulder. "Did he?"

Grady nodded.

"I'm glad." He paused for a moment, watching her eyes. She could have asked him then what he wanted. She could have asked if he loved her, but he let her go and was already moving toward the back of the barn.

"Jim's getting out of rehab tomorrow, he'll get physical therapy from home," he said over his shoulder. "I'm just going to grab some tools and I'll head over to Shauna's. The hospital bed they had to order won't fit through the door, I'll have to take the frame off."

Maybe when he came home they'd talk, she thought.

He stopped and turned around and came back, fishing something out of the back pocket of his jeans. "Here," he said, handing her her driver's license. Justice Mullens wanted you to have this back. He's officially dropping the charges Opie filed against you. You're free."

That was the thing. She didn't want to be.

The next day Grady had Thane drive her to her father's cabin, so she could pick up the Jaguar that had been sitting there since the day she'd been arrested. Cal had cleared the site. The cabin was gone, the burned-out shed was gone. Only the mangled dock remained. She stood with Thane at its edge. She didn't know what she'd do with the property. Her home now was on the other side of the lake, wasn't it?

She turned to him, took a deep breath to ask him, but he was already speaking.

"You're okay, here? I promised Shauna I'd help her get Jim settled."

Grady nodded and watched him go. He yanked hard at the door handle of the truck, it was the only way it would open, and then he got in and pulled out without looking back at her.

Grady turned to the lake to hear what the waves had to say to the bulkhead. Goodbye, goodbye, they seemed to whisper.

Impulsively, she pulled out her cellphone. Reception was bad and she stepped out carefully onto the uneven dock. Her mother answered on the last ring.

They were careful with each other, it was like a conversation between two strangers.

"Why are you calling?" her mother finally asked.

"I won't stand in your way, about the cabin. I mean the property. You can do with it what you want," Grady said.

"Oh." Her mother hadn't been prepared for that, she could tell by the long silence. "I know it's hard for you to believe, Grady, but I have happy memories up there. I just... I'm not a girl scout. I don't want a mansion there, but I wouldn't mind being comfortable."

"I understand," Grady said, although she didn't really, but she was trying.

"I'm glad you called," her mother went on. "This thing you got involved in, Grady, it's not too late to get out of, you don't have to be stuck there. You don't have to make the same mistake I did."

"Dad was not a mistake!" Grady said. "Didn't you love him at all?"

"Grady, that's not what I meant," she said after another long pause. "We loved each other in our own way. He loved me enough to want me to be happy. He would have wanted you to be happy, too Grady. It's not too late to get out of this thing with Thane. Even if— especially if— you're pregnant, we can—"

Her mother's voice had already been hard to understand, now the reception was lost completely. The two of them had never really understood each other. This thing with Thane was her marriage! Some of the old anger surfaced in Grady as she thought back to what her mother had said, that her father had been a mistake, but no, that's not what she'd said exactly, was it? 'Don't make the same mistake I did. Even if you're pregnant.'

Grady's father hadn't been her Mom's mistake. Grady had been the mistake. They'd gotten married because of her, stayed together because of her, been unhappy because of her.

How could she not have seen that? All her 23 years? Grady stood there for the longest time, long enough for the waves to change their tune again. Foolish, foolish they said as they slapped the bulkhead.

When she could trust her legs again, Grady got into the Jag and pulled away, so deep in thought she didn't look back. She made her first stop at the bank in town where she was given some temporary checks on her now full account. While there she opened accounts for Shauna's and Jim's two boys and put enough in them to pay for their first few years of college. Then she stopped at the municipal center where she paid off Thane's overdue property tax, along with Dan Hardin's. Then she drove to Glens Falls, and traded in the Jag for a Tundra with an extended cab.

It was late when she came home. Thane met her at the door to the cabin.

"Where were you?" he asked.

"Shopping," she said.

He glanced at the clock on the kitchen wall.

"Do you have somewhere to be?"

"Not any more, the lawyer will be closed by now," he said.

She was too excited about her own surprise, she didn't take the time to ask him what he needed a lawyer for. "I want to show you something," she said.

He nodded absently. "I need to show you something too," he said picking up a Manila folder from his desk.

"Can it wait?"

He shrugged. "Another day won't matter I guess."

He put the folder into the top drawer and let her lead him out of the cabin, up the steep path to the drive.

"Do we have company?" he asked as his eyes roved over the Tundra.

"No."

"Whose truck is this?"

"Yours."

His mouth turned down. "What do you mean mine?"

"I bought it for you today."

"I don't need a new truck."

"Yes you do. The seatbelts and the radio don't work any more in the Ranger, and it's at least 15 years old."

He stared at her.

"It's just a truck," she said.

"A truck that I didn't earn. I don't want it Grady."

"But Thane, I can afford it. It's more comfortable, you can haul more furniture in it."

"But it's not the Ranger."

"It's better than the Ranger."

"Did it ever occur to you that maybe I like things the way they were?"

Grady went silent as her heart heard what he left off, that he liked things the way they were without her.

Her mother had told her not to make a mistake, that she didn't have to stay with Thane if she didn't want to. But she wanted to stay with him. So much! But it mattered, too, what he wanted. He had never told her to go. She knew he wouldn't be the kind of man to make her leave. But he had never asked her to stay, either.

He came closer to her now and put a hand on her arm. "Listen, Grady, I appreciate what you're trying to do, but you don't need to do it. I don't want you to do it. We need to talk about what's yours and mine, and ..."

He stopped speaking as he noticed the paper in her hand, the receipt for taxes paid on the property, his property.

He sighed. "I was going to take care of that," he said through gritted teeth.

"I didn't want you to have to worry about it."

"It's mine to worry about, though, don't you see?"

"No, I don't." But she was starting to. He didn't want this to be a partnership, a true marriage.

Chapter Sixteen

Grady had been working all morning in the barn. Thane had come out, given her a quick goodbye and had driven off—in his old Ranger with Beau beside him. Was he serious about not wanting the new truck?

She thought about it all morning until she finally stopped for lunch, which wasn't really a break, since she took a call from a customer who wanted to change the specs on a cabinet Thane was building. As she hung up, the phone rang again.

On the other end was a woman's voice she didn't recognize. "This is John Silver's office. The papers your husband asked us to prepare are ready for your signatures. You can come in anytime. I don't think you have to come in together."

"What kind of papers?" Grady asked slowly.

"Umm, let me see. Looks like, umm, I see a plea bargain, no that's not it, looks like a separation agreement."

Grady didn't say anything. In the silence the woman's voice said, "It looks like there's a note here that says I can send them to you, but wait, I think they have to be notarized. Let me check, I'll call you right back."

Grady didn't hang up the phone for a long time, it was the only thing she had to hold on to.

John Silver looked up as his niece entered his office without knocking. Her hair was blue today. She was a pretty girl, but the ring in her nose always made him wince and look away.

"Do these have to be notarized, or can I just send them and they send them back?" she asked.

John took the folder from her ringed hand and repressed a sigh as his eyes flicked to his desk calendar and he calculated how many more days were left in her summer vacation.

"Where did you find these?"

"In the filing cabinet."

"These aren't the ones I was talking about. The papers to form a limited liability company are on your desk, with Thane and Grady McMasters signing as equal partners."

"There was something called a DBA."

John pinched the bridge of his nose. "That's 'doing business as.' They need to sign that too, that's all part of it. Just call and have them both come in, it will just avoid a lot of confusion."

He didn't realize confusion could no longer be avoided.

The call went to Thane's answering machine. "Sorry Mrs. McMasters, those weren't separation papers you needed to sign, it's a limited company or something like that, and my uncle said you and Mr. McMasters should both come in and sign."

Grady would have understood what she meant by limited company, if she'd only been there to hear it.

Thane felt the emptiness of the cabin, knew something was wrong, before he even heard Beau's worried whine. He went upstairs. Everything of Grady's was gone, her overnight bag, the clothes Thane had bought her. He went downstairs to his desk looking for a note. There was none. But she had placed the little figure of Beau that Thane had carved carefully on the center of the desk. He picked it up. Last time she ran, she had taken it with her. This time it seems she was leaving it behind. She was leaving them behind. And Thane had no idea why.

Out of habit, he hit the blinking button on the phone. As he listened to the message from John Silver's office, he understood why Grady had run. What he couldn't understand was why she didn't know Thane enough to think it was a misunderstanding. For a moment, he felt nothing, and then he pulled his arm back and threw the carving hard against the closest wall.

He went up to the barn searching for some clue, but all he discovered was Grady had left in a hurry. She hadn't cleaned up her tools, everything was left as if she had just taken a break and would be back in a minute.

He pulled his cellphone from his pocket and dialed her number. It rang for a while, which meant she wasn't out of range, yet. All he could do was leave a message.

"Grady, this whole thing is a misunderstanding," he began. "Those aren't separation papers I wanted you to sign," he said more gruffly than he meant. "Silver's assistant must have gotten them mixed up. I asked him to draw up papers for a limited liability company. If you'd come back, I can explain it all. Damn it, Grady, you can't just run away anytime there's a problem. You can't do this to me. I need you."

He was cut off by a beep. He hadn't meant to sound so angry, but damn it, that's how he felt. He threw his phone down on the work bench, and looked at the open toolbox. He gave it a good kick and sent the contents flying into the sawdust on the floor. Beau didn't bother to raise his head, just thumped his tail once tiredly .

"That's how you take care of your stuff, I ain't surprised you can't hang onto anything, or anybody." Dan Hardin's voice behind him was hard.

Thane turned and looked at the old man. "Not now, Dan."

"Now's as good a time as any. Where's Grady?"

"Wish I knew."

"You finally drove her away."

"It was a misunderstanding."

"Yeah, you not understanding how to treat a woman."

"Don't tell me one more time to apologize to her, I told you it wasn't anything I did."

"What else didn't you do?"

"What do you mean?"

"Did you tell her you wanted her to stay? That you loved her?"

"What do you know about love?"

Dan fingered the ring on his old hand. "Used to know more, but I guess I'm out of practice a long time. But I know a heap about being lonely. If I were you, I'd be going after her."

"I have no idea where she went. She doesn't want to be found."

"You're right," Dan said. "Not the part about her not wanting to be found. The part about you having no damned idea."

"So, what? I just magically guess where she went, and ask her nicely to come home?"

"You turn up every stone looking for her, and forget the asking. You tell her to come home where she belongs."

"You don't understand women."

"Neither do you."

Thane watched his neighbor turn his back and start shuffling back up the road. His shoulders seemed a little more hunched than usual.

When his cellphone rang, Thane almost dropped it in his hurry to answer it. It wasn't Grady. It was the jeweler in Glens Falls telling him the garnet necklace they had ordered was ready. The woman on the other end was about to hang up.

"Wait," Thane said. "The saleswoman took my ring size last time I was there, and I think you have the size of the garnet ring I brought in. I'd like to order wedding bands."

"Wouldn't you want to come in and look at them?"

"I don't have the time." He'd be too busy looking for Grady. "They don't have to be fancy, just give me something that will last a long time.

"When would you like them?"

"As soon as possible," he said as he hung up. He looked around the barn. What was he in such a hurry for? If he didn't find Grady, he'd have the wedding rings and no bride.

Grady was half-way to Lake Placid when her phone rang. She pulled off Route 73 and watched the phone vibrate in the passenger's seat. She didn't pick it up until the call went to message.

It had been a misunderstanding, she heard Thane say. Hadn't it been from the start?

"I need you, Grady," he had said. She heard all that, but she didn't hear the thing that would bring her back. He needed her. But did he want her? She and Thane worked well together. Slept well together. But sex and love weren't always the same thing. She had fallen in love with him. And Thane? She had fallen into his lap. He cared about her, sure, but he cared about a lot of people.

Grady from her first breath hadn't been wanted. She craved it, burned for it, and she wouldn't stay where she couldn't have it. She would never ever be someone's mistake again.

Thane couldn't file a missing person report, not if Grady had left of her own accord, but he went to the authorities, anyway, in this case to State Trooper James Oplin, who was propped up in a hospital bed at home, his leg in a cast from hip to toe. Justice Mike Mullens was there sitting at his bedside.

Without a word, Thane removed the wedding band from his finger and handed it to the judge.

"So, it didn't work out after all," Mike said as he took it and studied it. "I'm sorry, Will, I tried," he said in low tired voice.

"Who the hell is Will?" Opie asked.

Mike put the ring back on his finger and looked at it. "Will Henderson—Grady's father. He and I were close. He knew he was dying. He knew she'd run. He asked me to catch her."

"So you're the one her father called Moose," Thane said not able to keep the anger out of his voice. "She knew of you, but she didn't know you. Why the hell didn't you tell her?"

"She's not the kind of woman who responds well to being told what to do."

"Why the hell didn't you at least tell us?" Jim asked. "It would have made things easier."

"Would it have?" The justice shrugged. "I think she needed someone to be angry with, Opie, and I couldn't think of anyone she'd love to hate as much as you."

Jim smiled. "Thank you."

"Don't mention it." Then he looked back to Thane. "I'm sorry I got you into this, son."

"Well you're going to help get me out."

"You're already out aren't you? She left you, you're in the clear."

"What if I don't want to be?"

The justice smiled glumly, nodded as if in approval and then tilted his head in thought. "The charges were dropped against her, I don't know what we could do."

"Freeze her assets, close her credit cards," Thane said.

The judge looked at him. "That would be a bit unethical."

"Like remanding her to my care in the first place? You dropped the charges against her related to the shed burning on her property, but she got some big speeding tickets that day. Silver said they were bad enough she could lose her license."

The judge got up. "Let me see what I can do. "

"Hand me the phone," Jim said. "I'll contact every trooper from here to the Canadian border. I'll track her down, use handcuffs if I have to." He paused then. "But here's the question, buddy, what will you do with her once we find her? How are you going to make her stay?"

"Marry her for real."

Chapter Seventeen

Thane reserved the small stone church in Garnet Lake for Saturday. That gave him a week, but it was proving harder to find Grady than they thought. Jim had been able to access her records. She'd taken out a large sum from her account in Garnet Lake when she'd left and hadn't used a credit card since.

Shauna had volunteered to get the word out about the hasty wedding, since it was too late to send invitations. Thane's mother volunteered to do everything else. Shauna knew Grady had run. His mother thought Grady was back on Long Island visiting family, and he didn't bother to correct her.

Thane didn't think about what would happen if he didn't find Grady. He spent most of his time in the barn assembling furniture, but almost every piece had been touched by Grady, turned into a piece of art. He never should have sold the bed they'd made. They should have brought it home from the competition and made it their own, like he'd made Grady his own. Or tried to. Why didn't she see that? Why didn't she see that he loved her?

By Thursday, he'd finished up a couple of orders and went through some paperwork to see about scheduling deliveries. The couple who had bought the bedframe had ordered a nightstand to go with it. Thane called them, but instead of telling them the nightstand was ready, he asked to buy back the bed instead. It didn't take long to negotiate. It didn't fit in their guest room anyway. It was still in pieces. Like his marriage.

They wouldn't be available until Friday evening for him to pick it up. It would be cutting things close, unless Grady never showed up. Then he'd have all the time in the world. Then he'd want to be any place else but in Garnet Lake.

Grady drove first to Lake Placid and stayed at the most expensive resort. The tourists were too relaxed, the wait staff too cheery. She climbed Mount Marcy. She felt a bit of peace at the top, but she had to come down and when she did she felt heavier than before. She moved on to smaller towns, staying at ramshackle hotels that always seemed to have the word pine or tamarack in them. She wanted to be alone.

But that wasn't exactly true. She wanted to be alone with Thane. She wanted so much to be wanted.

On the fifth day she got her wish.

She checked out of a dingy hotel in Ogdensburg and threw her overnight bag in the bed of the Tundra.

The cab of the truck was so tall, she didn't see the state troopers until they stepped out from behind it. With their uniforms and crew cuts they looked like twins.

"Nice truck," one of them said as he approached.

"Drive's nice," she agreed, putting her hand on the door.

"Could I see your license?" the other asked.

"Why?"

The troopers exchanged a glance and did she imagine a smirk?

"Because I asked nicely."

Grady fished in her backpack for her wallet, removed the license and handed it over. He looked at it, then glanced at his partner as he slipped her license into the pocket of his uniform shirt. Did they exchange a nod?

"What's this all about?" Grady protested.

"You're wanted."

"Listen, the charges against me have all been dropped."

"Seems you're driving on a suspended license. You had some hefty speeding tickets you never paid. How fast can you get this truck to go by the way?"

She ignored the question. "I thought that was all taken care of."

The trooper shrugged. He took her keys from her hand. "Would you turn around please and place your hands on the hood of the truck?"

"This has got to be a mistake."

"Maybe it was a mistake for me to ask you so nicely," the trooper said in a serious tone.

Grady looked from one to the other and turned to face the truck.

The taller trooper moved in and with his boot knocked her right foot farther from her left, causing her to lean on the hood for balance.

His partner watched with folded arms. "Better watch out, heard she's got an arm on her."

"This has got to be a mistake," she said again. "Do you know Jim Oplin?"

"Do you?"

"He's a friend of mine."

"Would he say the same?"

"Well, I ... I saved his life."

"Did you now," the trooper said as he removed her one hand from the hood and then the other and cuffed them behind her. "You ought 'a get a medal."

He led her back to the patrol car and put her in the back and then pulled out of the parking lot of the hotel. She turned to watch his partner get in her truck and follow.

"You're not going to get away with this," Grady said.

The trooper smiled amiably into the rearview mirror.

"Neither are you."

Thane picked up his cell phone on the first ring.

"We've got her," Opie said.

"Where was she?"

"Some motel up in Ogdensburg. It'll be a few hours before they make it back to Garnet Lake. You home yet?"

"Far from it, I'm on my way to West Islip."

Thane glanced at the digital display of the clock on the dash then back to the traffic in front of him on the southbound lane of the Throgg's Neck Bridge. He was at least an hour away from his destination and another four hours away from home, that was in the best of conditions. The skyline of Manhattan seemed to be holding up the heavy sky. "I won't be back until late tonight."

"What the hell am I going to do with her 'til then?"

"Just make sure she doesn't run."

"You're not driving while you're talking to me, are you, buddy?" Jim asked. "You could get a ticket for that."

"No." Thane said as the traffic in front of him ground to a halt.

Grady watched the scenery become more and more familiar as the trooper drove toward Garnet Lake. After a few minutes they left a side road and came to a stop in front of a modest two-story house she'd never seen before.

The trooper escorted her out of the car and up the gravel path and rang the bell, while the other parked the Tundra in the driveway, got out and joined them.

They stood there for a few minutes. Inside it sounded like something was being dragged across the floor.

The door opened and Jim Oplin stood leaning against the jamb looking winded, a cast running all the way up his leg.

"Guys, why'd you cuff her?" he said.

"You told us to."

"Oh yeah, that's right. Well you can take 'em off now."

They uncuffed her, and put her keys and license into Opie's open palm.

"I owe you one," Opie said.

"You sure you don't want us to stick around 'til you get backup?" one of them said with a smirk. "We heard she's tougher than she looks."

"Nah, the wife'll be home soon. She knows how to handle her."

He turned to Grady as they left. "Come on in, Princess."

"This is your doing?" she said as she followed him inside, noticing how he leaned heavily against a railing on the wall that Thane had probably installed.

"I'm only following orders."

"If Thane thinks..."

"Listen, that's the problem, he doesn't think. But believe it or not, this isn't about Thane or you. It's about those speeding tickets you never paid, or appealed. You missed an appearance Thursday in Claverack and Kinderhook. You could be sitting in some county jail for the weekend, if I hadn't called in a favor."

"Why did you?"

"Shauna got it into her head that she wants to get married again."

"She's leaving you?"

"Nobody leaves me, Princess. She wants to renew our vows. Something about a guy almost being killed really brings out the romance in chicks. Anyway, she wants you there tomorrow, so I had to drag my sorry cast around and find you. So come on in, I'm due for my pain meds soon and I get real mean if I don't take them." He settled himself with difficulty on the bed that had been set up in the middle of the living room. His face was grim and pale, but he made an effort to make his voice light. "Make yourself at home, Princess, but first do me a favor and grab me a beer, will ya?"

"I thought you needed to take your medication."

"Need something to wash it down with, don't I?"

Grady went to the kitchen, the fridge was covered with preschool art, the handle of the door was sticky. She saw the cans of Genesee, but closed the door and opened cabinet doors until she found a glass and she brought him back some water.

"You don't listen, do you?" Jim said shaking his head, but he took the glass, wincing as he reached for it, and took a big swig before he went on. "He looks awful without you, by the way. Just mopes around. I swear if you don't go back, he's gonna die."

"Thane?" Grady said with disbelief, worry and she was ashamed to admit it—hope.

"What?! No! I meant Beau."

"You're a bastard."

"Thank you, Princess."

Grady gritted her teeth. "You know I hate when you call me that."

He grinned. "Why do you think I do it?"

Grady didn't say anything. Opie talked to her the same gruff way he always had, but the anger behind it was gone. It was a lousy irony that she would finally start getting along with him just as her relationship with Thane was ending.

Grady looked away and through the front window saw Shauna's car pull up. She went to the front door to help with the grocery bags dangling from her friend's arms.

"Grady! Thank goodness. I was afraid we'd have to cancel the service for tomorrow," Shauna said as she entered the kitchen.

"You would've canceled without me?" Grady felt a lump in her throat.

Shauna cocked her head, and gave Grady a look, but before she could say anything, Jim yelled to her from the living room.

"Shauna! I need you right here, right now!"

"How'd you talk Mr. Romantic into renewing his vows?" Grady asked as Shauna threw her bags down in a huff.

"Mr. Romantic?! I never would have called him that. Trust me, I had nothing to do with it. It was all his idea."

"Shauna!!!"

"All right, I'm coming!" Over her shoulder, she added. "I'm sorry Grady that your Mom can't make it."

"You invited her, too?"

"Oh my gosh, Grady, I invited everyone I could think of."

"Shauna if you don't get in here, right now..." Jim's voice had gone up a notch.

"I'm coming!"

Jim made a slashing sound near his throat as Shauna entered the living room.

"Does your neck hurt you? I told you you shouldn't have been so stubborn and taken that brace off. I swear Jim, if you don't follow doctors' orders, I'll send you back to rehab myself."

Jim pulled Shauna near. "She doesn't know!"

"Doesn't know what?"

"That she's getting married tomorrow."

"How could she not know?"

164

"I told her you and I were renewing our vows."

"Why did you do that?"

"Because Thane's not back home yet, and he asked me to keep her here at all costs. Because if I told her the truth, I didn't know how she'd react. And if she runs, I can't catch her with this damn cast on."

Shauna laughed. She settled herself on the edge of the bed. "You know that's not a bad idea renewing our vows."

"I told you I'm only getting married once. I don't need to do it again."

"Why not, it would be romantic."

"You don't need romance when you've got real love."

"Actually romance every once in a while wouldn't hurt."

Jim pulled his wife forward and kissed her. "How's that for a start?"

He didn't get to hear how it would end, because his boys came careening into the living room.

Shauna sighed. "After this vow renewing is over, we need to talk about your vow of celibacy..."

Chapter Eighteen

Grady was happy for Shauna and she was trying hard to show it the next morning. She felt out of place, not just because she was the only one dressed and ready to go. She wore the light silk dress, with the barest of sleeves that Thane had bought off the rack for her in Glens Falls. The flower print was so delicate, that from a distance the dress looked white. It fit her perfectly, was fit for a wedding, except she wasn't the bride.

She played hairdresser now to Shauna in front of the bedroom mirror as her friend sat perched on the corner of her bed. She unclipped a hairpin for the third time and tried again to capture an unruly wisp of Shauna's hair. Shauna stopped her, took the pin from her hand and put it haphazardly into place.

"Here, I'll do that. It doesn't have to be perfect, Grady, just good enough." She stood up and indicated Grady should trade places with her. "Kind of like my marriage, huh?"

Grady didn't laugh. "You have everything," she said.

Shauna tugged at Grady's hair just short of painfully, pushing in pearl-tipped pins in a business-like manner. "I've got everything, all right. Maple syrup in my hair, a grape juice stain down my dress. My new dress! And I swear Jim gave me a hickey last night. Does it show?"

"I'm really happy for you, Shauna, I am."

"You're just sad for yourself," Shauna said as she brought her face down level with Grady's to admire her handiwork. "You'll have it all sooner than you think. Just let it come, Grady. Promise me?" Grady couldn't lie to those rich brown eyes, so she said nothing at all.

Thane was going to be late for his own wedding, a wedding that might not even take place. It had been long after midnight when he'd returned to the empty cabin. He had checked his messages, expecting, or at least hoping there'd be one from Grady. He could tell the way Beau cocked his head that the mutt expected it too. Beau had curled up in the corner next to the cold wood stove and had gone to sleep. Thane had gone to work in the loft, carefully nailing and assembling the bed, making a whole from the parts. The birch branches that stood like sentries on either side of the headboard touched the tongue and grooved pine of the ceiling, just clearing the roof purlins. He wanted to present it to Grady seamless and whole. Like their marriage should be.

Now he shoved his red toolbox under the bed frame and pulled his long-unused suit from the pine closet. As he knotted his tie, he admired the bed board and the scene of Ethan Ridge that had unfolded across it under Grady's hands. They had created this together, both their talents working with and against each other to create something better. And if she said yes to him today, this bed would be a metaphor. If she said no, his sole satisfaction would be in breaking it to bits.

Shauna drove them all to church in the minivan, Grady in the passenger's seat, the boys all the way in the back and Jim stretched out in the middle seat complaining about every pothole.

The parking lot was full and they had to park down the street. Grady couldn't understand why Jim had turned down Shauna's offer to drop him off right in front. As soon as the boys were unbuckled they ran out, with Shauna in pursuit. Jim held Grady back, and she had to help him get out of the van. He stood for a moment and scanned the sides of the street and the parking lot and she thought he cursed.

"What did you say?"

"Let's get this over with," he said.

"Gosh, you are romantic," she said as he put a hand on her shoulder and leaned heavily on it, even though he had a cane. It took a long time to reach the concrete steps of the church. He didn't seem ready to climb them yet and she stood with him as he caught his breath. The metal railing burned under her hand. Up the block she read the movie title off the theater marquee. The letters were crooked. The white paint on the post office was peeling. The bank's sign missed a letter and commanded its customers to "Dive through."

She found fault wherever she could, but it wasn't easy, because despite its rough edges Garnet Lake had charm, and it was still going to be hard to see this all in her rearview mirror for the last time when she drove away again. Except she remembered Jim had never returned her license.

It didn't matter, she knew the bus stopped in front of the post office. As she stood there planning her escape, which felt more like an exile, guests started to arrive. Some of the faces, like Cal's, were familiar, others strange, and had she been paying more attention it might have surprised her that some of them commented on how beautiful she looked.

Robert, the bank manager, stopped for a moment, commented in his gentle way about the weather, before continuing. "Nice to see you're making it official Grady. Things started off kind of out of the ordinary, but the important thing is how they go along." He patted her on the shoulder before walking up the stairs into the church.

She turned. Jim looked at her now over the metal railing. The eyes that held hers were the eyes of a State Trooper, alert, focused and intense. She could tell he knew she wanted to make a run for it. And she could have. In his condition he could never catch her. And she would have, if the tightness in his jaw hadn't relaxed into a big smile that went all the way to his eyes. It took the hard edges off of him, and she saw suddenly what her friend Shauna loved about him: genuineness, loyalty and behind it all a boyish vulnerability. His smile dimmed a little and she could swear he blinked back a tear.

"If it weren't for you, Grady, my boys wouldn't have a father. I told Shauna I'd never leave her, but I came pretty close in that damned mine. Thank you. For saving my life."

"I," Grady began. "You're welcome," she said haltingly because he'd made her speechless.

She was so intent on his face that she didn't see his hands moving, didn't even see the glint of metal against sunlight. But she heard that all too-familiar clicking sound.

"That's three for three, Princess, in case you're keeping score,"

Opie said nonchalantly. She looked down, one silver bracelet was already around her wrist and he was attaching the other handcuff to the metal railing.

Grady swallowed every name she wanted to call him, as Thane's parents appeared in her field of vision. If her mother-in-law noticed that Grady's wrist was shackled to the metal railing as she gave her a quick hug, she didn't comment on it.

"Doesn't she look beautiful, Bob?" Marilyn McMasters asked of her husband. He grunted, nodded, looked pointedly at the handcuffs and then they were gone, blinking out of the sunlight and into the darkness of the church.

Opie stayed, standing with arms crossed like a bouncer.

"I hate you," Grady said.

He looked at her and cocked his head. "I think you did, but you don't any more, do you? Not after what we've been through. I'm part of your life now whether you like it or not. I'm the best man."

"You can't make me stay."

"I still have your license."

"I'll take the bus."

"To where? You won't find a better place."

"I don't belong here,"

"But you belong with Thane."

"Says who?"

Jim shook his head and pinched the bridge of the nose she had broken and he cursed under his breath. "Would he have gone through all this trouble if he didn't think so?"

"Well, he never said."

"You women spend too much time thinking over what's said and not said. Can't you just take us as we are and trust us a little? We grow 'em loyal up here Grady. You two might have started out as an accident, but maybe it was meant to be, karma or some crap like that. Why can't you just relax and let it happen?"

"Because it's not up to just me!"

"You're right," Thane said behind her. "It's up to me too."

Until that moment, pride had been like a leash around her heart.

As she turned and saw Thane, that leash snapped. The only thing that kept her from going to him was the cuff around her wrist ... and the fact that Thane didn't move to hold her.

The lines of his body were rigid and inaccessible in the dark suit he wore. Despite the distance between them, she saw tension in his jaw and mistrust in his brown eyes as he watched her.

He was standing beside his old Ranger, and he opened the passenger's side door to let Beau out. Grady knelt down to greet the dog, and his speed surprised her. He would have knocked her off balance had she not been chained to the railing. With one hand, she tried to calm him. Like her heart, he wouldn't be quieted.

When Thane pulled the truck in front of St. John's church and saw Grady waiting outside, he let himself hope for a moment that everything was coming together toward a happy end.

But there was something wrong with the scene. Jim's stance first of all: arms folded, legs locked, but not from the cast he wore the length of his leg. He was more bodyguard than best man. And Grady? She was staring down at her hands.

When she turned to him, he wasn't sure what he noticed first. How beautiful she was. How different her hair looked, pulled back away from her heart-shaped face. How slender her neck was. How the white dress she wore hugged the trim lines of the body he knew so well. How storm-wrecked her hazel eyes seemed. Or the circle of steel around her wrist.

Thane cursed inwardly, as he strafed his best friend with a look. "Do what it takes to get Grady to the church," Thane had said. "And to keep her there." He hadn't meant this.

He had let Beau out of the truck because it was too hot to leave him in the cab, and there was something desperate about the way he pawed the window. The old dog seemed to turn puppy as the door opened. There was nothing like resentment to slow him as he bounded up the steps. The dog could teach them both something about loyalty and honesty, Thane thought, as he followed more slowly.

He was surprised at the bitterness behind that thought. Seeing to what lengths Opie had gone to, only proved what lengths Grady had considered to escape.

Thane pulled Beau away from Grady with one hand and offered her his other to help her up. He released her as soon as she had regained her balance. Without taking his eyes from her, he reached out and caught the keys Jim threw in his direction.

"She's all yours, Buddy," Jim said, and then Thane was alone with his wife on the steps of the church.

But was she all his?

She avoided his eyes, looking at Beau instead who wagged his head expectantly between the two of them.

She held her wrist up for Thane to unlock the cuffs. He moved close enough to oblige, but hesitated. If he couldn't keep her for good, he could hold her long enough to get some answers.

"I know why you left, Grady," he said. "But what I can't understand is why you didn't come back. You got my message, didn't you? Those weren't separation papers I wanted you to sign. Silver's assistant got it all wrong. It was all a misunderstanding."

"That's what I'm afraid of." Her eyes were fixed on the knot of his tie.

He put his hand to her chin and angled her head up. Still she wouldn't meet his eyes.

"What do you mean, Grady?"

"It was a misunderstanding from the start. You got pushed into this. It was all a mistake. I don't want to be anyone's mistake."

"How could you think that?"

"You said you liked things the way they were. Before I came."

"I never said that!"

"Yes you did. When I bought you the truck."

"I wasn't talking about us Grady. There are some things you'll have to let me do for myself, like pay back my own debts, but we're in this together. Our future is together."

She didn't look at him, her posture was as rigid as ever. "Unless, you don't want to be married to me," he said slowly.

"I want it more than anything," she said, studying the cuff around her wrist.

"Then what's the matter?"

"I'm not sure about..."

"What? If you want to live here?"

"No, it's not that! I wouldn't want to be anywhere else, but, I'm not sure how you feel ... about me."

He took her by the shoulders. "I love you, Grady. How can you not know that? I thought it was so obvious. I could never take my eyes off you."

She looked at him finally. "I thought you were just watching me so I wouldn't get into any more trouble. And I thought maybe I was just convenient for you, because I was there."

"You will never be convenient, but that's who you are and I love you, Grady. I think I have from the start, from the moment you walked in front of that damned bulldozer, when you grabbed me by the collar and promised me you'd give me everything. You're going to make good on that promise, Grady."

The way her eyes narrowed and then closed, the way she sank against him then, told him she hadn't been sure of anything until this moment. "You'll make good on that promise, won't you?" he repeated.

"Yes," she whispered against his neck. He had the feeling she was answering all his questions. He asked them anyway, speaking them softly against her hair, inhaling her scent as he held her tightly against him.

"Do you want to marry me?" he asked.

"We *are* married."

"Do you want to stay married?"

"More than anything."

"You're never going to leave me again, are you?"

Grady lifted her head and shook it.

"Say it," he demanded softly.

"I'll never leave you again. I promise. I missed you so much. I hated being away from you." And then she couldn't talk as his mouth covered hers.

It was only when Thane heard the clearing of a throat behind them that he remembered he was standing on the steps of the church

He opened his eyes, but he didn't move his lips from Grady's. Just outside the door stood Dan Hardin in a black suit, short at the ankles, exposing his brown rubber boots.

Thane closed his eyes again, feeling Grady smile against his lips.

"Hmph. When you're good and ready, we'll be waiting for you. Or should I just have 'em start in on my funeral mass?" The old man tapped his cane a few times against the door then gave up, mumbling as he disappeared inside.

And then there was another voice, but less gruff. "I thought that part came at the end of the ceremony, but what do I know, I'm just the Justice of the Peace. I guess things were out of order from the first. Nice to see it still has a happy ending." Mike Mullens cleared his throat again. "Whenever you're ready Mr. and Mrs. McMasters, we'll get this started. Again."

It was already started and if it was up to Thane, it wouldn't end.

Thane let Grady go, but not until he was good and ready. Not until his wife's cheeks were flushed and a strand of her dark hair had come unraveled from its clip. Then he stepped away from her, pulled the garnet necklace from his suit pocket and fastened it around her neck. She picked it up with her free hand.

"It's beautiful!" she said. She pulled against the handcuff. "But it doesn't exactly match the rest of my jewelry," she said, looking at him expectantly. He unlocked the cuff from the metal railing. He didn't touch the cuff around her wrist.

"What are you doing?" Grady asked as he secured the metal around his own wrist, making a prisoner of both of them.

"Making sure you make good on your promise and don't run away."

He gave her one last kiss and closed his hand around hers. "We're in this together, Grady, you believe that, don't you?" She looked down at the handcuffs then back up to his eyes, and nodded.

"I believe in you," she said. And she had from the beginning.

The reception was over, but Grady's marriage was just beginning. It had been a simple party in the fire hall, but heartfelt and the congratulations sincere. She and Thane belonged to each other now, but they also belonged here to this community.

It was evening when they finally made it back home. Beau collapsed in the corner by the woodstove and started snoring gently. Grady looked around. The cabin was the same, but it felt different to be here. It felt right. She was no longer an invader or a guest or a prisoner. Thane took her hand and pulled her towards the stairs so quickly she lost her balance.

"What's your hurry?" she asked with a soft laugh. "We have all the time in the world."

"I want to show you something."

She gasped as she reached the loft and saw the bed Thane had made. The canopy of birch branches barely brushed the ceiling. It crowned the room, but didn't crowd it.

"I bought it back. They never even assembled it."

"It's beautiful," Grady said. "It fits perfectly. Like it grew here. Like it was always a part of the cabin."

She turned to him. "When I was working on it, I pictured it here." She put her hands to his tie and began to loosen it. "I pictured you in it. With me."

His fingers tangled themselves in her hair. "What did you picture?"

"I'll show you," she said, pulling him down to her so she could kiss him. He laid her down on the bed under the canopy of branches and suddenly she felt like she was in the shadows of the forest, a place she'd always felt safe.

"You saved me so many times," she whispered. "That makes me indebted to you for life, doesn't it?"

"That makes me responsible for you."

She shook her head.

"You are so stubborn," he said.

"So are you!" She rolled over onto him and began to undo the buttons of his shirt, began to pay back the debt she owed him by taking pleasure in the way his hands moved, grasping her hair at the back of her head, pulling her in for another kiss.

She was where she wanted to be, but it wasn't the place. She'd found her home in Thane and she could find her way back to him with her eyes closed.

Epilogue

The trees surrounding the cabin were on fire with fall when Mike Mullens came to visit Grady. It was coming up on a year since her father had died, and she was thinking again how little she had from him to remember him by.

When the Justice pulled up in his pickup, she was working in the barn, and she came to greet him as he stood in the dappled sunlight just outside the entrance.

"Thane's down by the lake, putting the canoe in," she said. "I'll go get him."

He shook his head. "I came to see you, Grady. I have something to give you."

He looked at the folded piece of paper in his hand for a moment and the corners of his mouth went down.

"What is it?" she asked, wondering if it had to do with the charges that were dropped against her all those months ago.

Without looking up, he handed her a letter.

She recognized her father's tight neat script. It was addressed to 'Moose.'

She looked up at the judge. "That's you?!"

He nodded.

"Why didn't you tell me you knew my Dad?"

He rubbed his forehead. "I don't know, Grady, maybe it was because I wasn't sure if I knew you. It was hard to reconcile the girl your Dad was so proud of with the woman who appeared before me in court."

She read a few lines and looked up again.

"Why didn't you tell me about this earlier?"

"I wasn't sure you'd be able to hear what he was really saying in that letter."

Her heart hung on every word her father had written, not to her, he had left no message behind, but about her.

'How do you put that much love into words,' he'd written. The letters swam, and she blinked.

She had concentrated so much on her father leaving her. This letter was about him loving her. And wanting what was best for her.

After a long moment she turned back to the judge. "How did you know remanding me to Thane's care would be the thing to keep me here?"

"I had no idea. I was desperate. All I knew is that he's a good man." He paused for a moment and put a hand on her shoulder. "And you're a good girl, Grady. Your Dad was always so proud. He still is. He'd be happy, you know. You should be too."

Grady wiped her tears with the back of her hand and looked out over the lake she loved so well, that never changed and still was somehow always different. "I am happy," she said. Sadness was a part of that too, the darkness under the surface, but it was no longer so deep, no longer something she could drown in.

She watched from a distance as Thane slid the canoe over the bulkhead and into the clear blue water. Then he turned and waved. "I'll be there," she called down.

The justice gave her a pat on the shoulder. "So will he, Grady. So will I. We'll be here for you."

She nodded. She would be here too, where she belonged. Carefully she folded the letter and gave it back to the judge. He began to protest, but she put a hand on his arm.

"It was for you. I have everything I need now," she said.

He looked at her closely and seemed to find what he was searching for, and he took his leave. She watched him go. Then she stepped out of the barn into the sunlight to join her husband.

Other Books by the Author
available as e-books and print copies at most online retailers

Home Sweet Stranger, by Adria Townsend
Contemporary full-length novel

Forced to flee East Germany as a young girl, Ellie Meyer returns after the fall of the Berlin Wall to reclaim her home, only to discover her childhood friend Luther Beck has made a claim of his own. To avoid a lengthy property dispute, they enter into an uneasy agreement to share the house. Even as Ellie's suspicions grow about Luther's role in her troubled past, so too does an underlying attraction. As she uncovers his secrets, she'll find that her heart might be the biggest traitor of all.

To Conquer the Heart of a King, under the name J. S. Laurenz
Historical novella

Before Lukas of Falkenberg returns to the Black Forest to take the throne from his dying father, he pays a visit to the nameless Seer at the Cloister of Mariendorf. He takes her captive using her intuition to establish his reign. She willingly trades the punishing confines of the cloister for a palace prison in the hope of gaining her ultimate freedom. Although blind, she can see what the future king cannot—the needs of his subjects. She will win them over, but can she conquer the heart of a king before his half-brother Magnus separates them in a plot even she cannot foresee?

Reviews Appreciated:
Thank you for reading A Remote Chance. If you've enjoyed the book, would you consider rating it and reviewing it at the site where it was purchased?

Questions, comments, or to sign up for a mailing list for new releases: Please visit my blog, http://dime-store-cowgrrl.blogspot.com or contact me at WholeOtherStory@gmail.com

A Remote Chance is dedicated to Sue W.

Thanks first to Suzanne, my editor and friend. I'm so grateful our story continues. Thanks to Bibi Wein for allowing me to make her my mentor. The town of Garnet Lake is a fictional place based on small towns located in the Adirondack Park in upstate New York. There are some real lakes called Garnet, but I've never been to them, and the lake here is fictional based on the many lakes found throughout the park. Although some memorable people have sparked my imagination and may have inspired certain expressions, mannerisms, or circumstances, no character represents a real person except Dan Hardin, whose name I changed, but I hope those who knew him will recognize 'the Farmer' and his creative vocabulary. Neighbor has a different meaning in the park, and tough weather and circumstances cause you to rely on each other, and we've had the best. James Oplin was born from witnessing the "Trooper smiles" of real state troopers I know, the way they refer to their grim expressions captured in Academy graduation photographs. I have never known a trooper to curse like James Oplin, or conduct themselves with anything other than decorum. Thanks to B.I.L. for stories about law enforcement. Stratford on Hudson gave me insight into creating scenes beyond the theater, and above all encouragement. The Wells House inspired The Well. Todd C., being offered a shiner for his help, inspired one of the scenes. Thanks to the Adirondack Center for Writing and their many resources and network. Thanks to Alma, Sharon and Wendy at the library that was my lifeline. Thanks to the Adirondack Museum. Thanks to The Albany Times Union, Adirondack Life, The Glens Falls Chronicle, North Country Public Radio, and Nancy O' for allowing me to give voice to other stories. Local artisans and their rustic furniture inspired the carpentry. Thanks to my parents. Shawn accompanied me again in this book. Thanks to my book club pals for suggestions and support. Thanks to Bill, Doris, Kathy and George for access to the lakes and for lots of laughs. To Dave, whose years in construction inspired Thane's character, thank you for building our fortress of solitude in the Adirondacks and to A and E for filling it with fun.

About the Author

Adria Townsend splits her time between the Adirondacks in New York and Pennsylvania where she teaches German at a university. She is a freelance writer for *The Albany Times Union* and *Adirondack Life Magazine*. Her articles have appeared in *The San Francisco Chronicle*, *The Miami Herald,* and *The Charlotte Observer*. She is a commentator for North Country Public Radio and has been interviewed by New Hampshire Public Radio about her book, To Conquer the Heart of a King, and the wild west of electronic publishing. Her creative nonfiction has appeared in Syracuse University's journal Stone Canoe.

Adria Townsend also writes under the name J. S. Laurenz and blogs at http://dime-store-cowgrrl.blogspot.com

Made in the USA
Middletown, DE
09 July 2016